THE PROOF

THE PROOF

César Aira

Translated by
Nick Caistor

SHEFFIELD – LONDON

First published in 2017 by And Other Stories
Sheffield – London
www.andotherstories.org

Originally published in Spanish by Grupo Editor Latinoamericano, Buenos Aires, in 1992 as *La Prueba*.

9 8 7 6 5 4 3 2 1

ISBN 978-1-908276-96-4
eBook ISBN 978-1-908276-97-1

Editors: Luke Brown and Tara Tobler; Proofreader: Sarah Terry; Typesetter: Tetragon, London; Typefaces: Linotype Swift Neue and Verlag; Cover Design: Edward Bettison; Printed and bound by TJ International Ltd, Padstow, Cornwall, UK.

A catalogue record for this book is available from the British Library.

This translation has been selected to receive financial assistance from English PEN's PEN Translates programme, supported by Arts Council England. English PEN exists to promote literature and our understanding of it, to uphold writers' freedoms around the world, to campaign against the persecution and imprisonment of writers for stating their views, and to promote the friendly co-operation of writers and the free exchange of ideas. www.englishpen.org

This book was also supported using public funding by Arts Council England.

Supported using public funding by
ARTS COUNCIL ENGLAND

ENGLISH PEN

MIX
Paper from responsible sources
FSC® C013056

THE PROOF

'Wannafuck?'

Marcia was so startled she didn't understand the question. She looked hastily around her to see where it came from . . . Yet it wasn't so very out of place, and perhaps nothing else was to be expected, here in this labyrinth of voices and glances that were transparent, light, inconsequential and yet at the same time dense, rapid, slightly wild. But if you went around expecting something . . .

Three blocks before Plaza Flores, on this side of the avenue a youthful world came alive. Stationary but mobile, three-dimensional, it defined its own boundaries, the volume it created. There were big groups of boys and girls – more of the former – gathered in the doorways of the two record shops, in the empty area round the Cine Flores that stood between them, and clustered against the parked cars. At this time of day they were out of school and all met up here. She had also left school two hours earlier (she was in year ten), but a long way away, fifteen blocks further down, in Caballito. She was out for her daily walk. Marcia was overweight and had a back problem that wasn't serious then at the age of sixteen, but might become so in the future. No one had told her she should walk; she did it out of a therapeutic instinct. For other reasons as well, above all habit; she had survived a serious depression she had suffered, which had reached its climax a few months earlier, by being constantly on the move, and now she still was, just because, out of inertia or superstition. By this stage of her exercise, already close to the point where she turned around, it was as though she were slowing down; after the kilometre of no man's land on Avenida Rivadavia which separated the two districts, invading this new, youthful space made her go increasingly slowly, even though she did not slacken her pace.

She came up against floating signs; every step, every swing of her arms met endless responses and allusions... with its sprawling youthful world, arriving in Flores was like raising a mirror to her own history, only slightly further from its original location – not far, easily reachable on an evening walk. It was only logical that time should become denser when she arrived. Outside her story she felt she was gliding along too rapidly, like a body in the ether where there was no resistance. Nor should there be too much, or she would be paralysed, as had happened to her during the rather tragic period that was already vanishing into the past.

Although it was only seven o'clock, it had already grown dark. It was winter, and night fell early. Not dark night; that would come later. In the direction she was walking, Marcia had the sunset in front of her; at the far end of the avenue there was an intense red, violet and orangey glow she could only see as she drew closer to Flores and Rivadavia made a gentle bend. It was still almost daytime when she set out, but the light faded quickly; in midwinter it would have been dark by half past six, but the season had moved on and these were no longer what you could call the shortest days of the year, although it was still cold, twilight descended quickly, and nightfall was already in the air when school was out at five. There must still have been light in the atmosphere, even at seven o'clock, but the street was so brightly lit that the sky looked dark by comparison. Especially when she reached the more commercial part of Flores, near the square, with the illuminated shop windows and canopies. This made the red glow of the sunset in the distance seem incongruous, although it was no longer red, more like a weak blue shadow with grey streaks around it. Here the brightness of the mercury lights was dazzling, perhaps because of the crowd of young people who were looking at each other and talking, waiting or arguing loudly. In the previous blocks where there were fewer people (it was very cold, and those who weren't young, with their ridiculous need to meet their friends, preferred to stay indoors), the lights appeared less bright; although it was true it had been earlier in the evening when she passed them by. Time seemed to be going backwards, from an unknown midnight, towards evening, towards day.

She didn't feel it, or shouldn't have felt it, because she herself was part of the system, but all those young people were wasting their time. The system meant being happy. That was what it was all about, and Marcia understood that perfectly, even though she couldn't be part of it. Or thought she couldn't. However that might have been, she entered the enchanted realm, which was not in any particular spot, but was rather a fortuitous moment of the evening. Had she reached it? Or had it reached her? Had it been waiting for her? She didn't ask herself any more questions, because she was already there. She had forgotten she was walking, that she was going in a certain direction (she wasn't headed anywhere anyway) through the soft resistance of the light and darkness, silence and the glances exchanged between face and face.

They looked at each other, met one another: that was why they were out on the street. They talked, shouted, whispered secrets among themselves, but everything quickly dissolved into nothing. That was the joy of finding oneself in a particular place and moment. Marcia had to sidestep to skirt round groups inside which a secret was circulating. The secret was being young or not. Even so, she couldn't help looking, seeing, paying more attention. Boys and girls were constantly peeling off the little groups, scurrying this way and that, in the end always to return, talking, gesticulating. They filled all this stretch of the avenue; they seemed to be constantly coming and going, but the number remained the same. They gave an impression of shifting sociability. In fact, it was as if they weren't stationary but were just passing through, exactly as she was. It wasn't a place of resistance, except a poetic, imaginary one, but a gentle tumult of loud and soft laughter. They all seemed to be arguing. Arsehole! Arsehole! was the commonest insult, although nobody ever came to blows. They accused each other of all sorts of things, but that was just their way. They did not watch her go by; they weren't silent or immobile enough for that. Besides, it was only an instant, a few metres. She walked on, crossing Calle Gavilán, where she hit the real crowds. This side of the intersection, where the huge Duncan café stood, was darker. There seemed to be a lot more people here. Now they were typical kids from Flores: long hair, leather jackets, motorbikes parked on the pavement. Latent urgency hung in the air. There was a closed newspaper stand, with a florist's next to it; there were small knots of teenagers for a further twenty or thirty metres, right up to the first entrance to the shopping mall; it was outside the record shop there that the number of youngsters displaying themselves reached its height, for the moment at least. Marcia knew that on the next corner, opposite a pharmacy, at this time of evening there was always a gaggle of kids. She was venturing into the most typical part of the neighbourhood. For now, though, she was still on the previous corner, by the Duncan café, packed with bikers . . . Marcia could already hear music from the record shop: The Cure, whom she loved.

The music changed her mood, took her to its silent conclusion. As this had not happened with the music from the two earlier record shops, it must have been down to how good it was, although possibly it was the climax of the accumulated impressions. The music was the remaining resistance needed to make the mall completely fluid. Every look, every voice she slipped past, mingled with the night. Because it was night. The day was over and night was in the world; at this hour in summer it was still broad daylight, but now it was night. Not the kind of night for sleeping, the real one, but a night superimposed on the day because it was winter.

She was walking along enveloped in her halo, in her sixteen years. Marcia was blonde, small, chubby, somewhere between child and adult. She was wearing a woollen skirt and a thick blue pullover, with lace-up shoes. Her face was flushed from her walk, but it was always ruddy anyway. She knew her movements made her seem out of place; she could have been just another member of one of the gangs or other, where girls like her were not infrequent, chatting and laughing, but she didn't know anyone in Flores. She looked like a girl who was going somewhere and had to pass through here. It was a miracle no one had handed her any fliers; she was given them every day, but for some strange reason not this time; all the people handing them out had been looking the other way when she passed. It was as if she were a ghost, invisible. But that only made her increasingly the empty centre of everyone's gaze and conversations . . . if they could be called conversations. If nothing was aimed at her, it was because all directions had vanished. It was a swarm of unknown youngsters . . .

'Hey, I'm talking to you . . . '

'To me?'

'Wannafuck?'

Two girls had split off from the large group or groups outside the Duncan, and they began to follow her. It was not too long before they caught up, because Marcia wasn't far ahead. One of them was talking, the other was her sidekick, listening eagerly a few steps behind. When eventually she had made out who was speaking, Marcia came to a halt and looked at her:

'Are you mad?'

'No.'

They were two punks, dressed in black. Very young, although maybe slightly older than she was, with pale, childish features. The one doing the talking was very close to her.

'You're gorgeous and I want to fuck you.'

'Are off your head?'

She glanced at the other one, who was the same and looked very serious. It didn't seem like a joke. She didn't know them, or at least couldn't recognise them beneath their disguises. There was something serious but crazy about the pair of them, about the situation. Marcia couldn't get over her astonishment. She looked away and carried on walking, but the punk grabbed her by the arm.

'You're the one I've been waiting for, you fat cow. Don't make things difficult. To begin with, I want to lick your cunt!'

Marcia freed herself at once, and yet turned her head to answer her a second time.

'You're nuts.'

'Come to the dark bit,' she said, pointing to Calle Gavilán, which was in fact pitch black, lined with huge trees. 'I want to kiss you.'

'Leave me in peace.'

She set off again, and the two stood where they were, apparently giving up before they started, but the one talking was raising her voice, as people always do to somebody walking away, even when they are still close by. Vaguely alarmed, Marcia realised a posteriori that this stranger had been speaking loudly right from the start, and that some of the others had heard her and were laughing. Not just the youngsters, but the flower seller as well, an elderly man, a grand-dad, whom Marcia brushed past in her flight. He was looking on with great interest, but did not allow it to show on his face, as if he were not entitled to react. He would do so later, when he talked to his female customers; there would be no stopping him with his 'degenerates', his 'you won't guess what happened', et cetera. 'They must have been on drugs,' the old ladies would say. How thoughtless these girls were, Marcia was surprised to find herself thinking. How reckless! How they undermined youth! The boys who had heard didn't seem to care in the slightest about that; they were laughing and shouting, thinking it was great.

The two punks were some way away. Without meaning to, Marcia had sped up a little. The music was louder, and some boys standing in the record store doorway a bit further on were looking at her curiously. They might not have heard, but could have guessed, if not the exact meaning of what was going on, at least how strange it was. Or perhaps she wasn't the first person those two had approached, or others: maybe it was a joke in bad taste they made the whole time. She didn't turn to look, but guessed that the two punks had rejoined one of the small groups and were laughing as they waited for their next victim.

A few more steps, and Marcia had reached the loudest spot. But now the music had changed meaning. It was as though it had become real, something that never happened with music. And that reality prevented her from hearing it. She too was thinking at her loudest, so that it was also as if her thinking had become real. Where she was now there were still clusters of youngsters, who as before no longer paid her any attention (the entire incident had lasted only a few seconds, it was almost as if she had not stopped), but now they were no longer emblems of beauty or happiness, but of *something else.*

Everything had changed. Marcia was shaking from delayed shock. Her heart was in her mouth. She was dumbstruck with astonishment, although, as she didn't usually talk to herself, this wasn't obvious. But the effect was already wearing off, had worn off. The shock had a delayed effect because there had been no time for it while the event was taking place; but afterwards it made no sense, it was a fictional shock. Marcia wasn't hysterical, or even nervous or impressionable, or paranoid; she was quite calm and rational.

No, that wasn't where the change was. The atmosphere, the weight of reality had changed. Not because it had become more or less real, but because it seemed that now, anything could happen. Wasn't it like that before? Before, it was as though nothing could happen. It was the system of beauty and happiness of the young people. It was the reason why they gathered there at that time of day, it was their way of making the neighbourhood, the city, the night, real. All of a sudden all of them were different, as if a cloud of gas had suddenly been released. It was incredible how everything could change, thought Marcia, even the smallest details. There was no need for catastrophes or cataclysms . . . On the contrary, an earthquake or a flood would be the surest way of keeping things as they were, of preserving values.

That two girls, two women, should have wanted to pick her up, out loud, voicing obscenities, two punks who confirmed their violent self-expulsion from proper behaviour . . . It was so unexpected, so novel . . . Really, anything could happen, and those who could make it happen were the hundreds of young people who came out into the street to waste time at nightfall, after school. They could do anything. They could make night fall in broad daylight. They could set the world spinning, and infinitely slow down Marcia's walk in a straight line (apart from where there was a bend in Rivadavia) from Caballito to Flores.

Marcia was one of those girls of her age who could swear that they are victims. Even though they're not, they could swear it. Maybe that was why they had picked her out. There are not many of her kind, even though there are a lot of virgins. A virgin is surrounded by an atmosphere filled with possibilities, looks, time, messages . . . If she doesn't appear to be one, then the atmosphere is purer, more transparent, everything flows that much more quickly. If she does look like one, as was Marcia's case, one in a million, that atmosphere can burst into reality. All the faces round her, all the floating, self-absorbed, exhibitionist bodies had become weighted with stories and possibilities for stories, like she was wandering through myriad tales . . .

She had not taken five steps and she was already completely calm again. In her heart she felt something like the shadow of euphoria: that is the infallible effect of reality. She raised her eyes and all the lights of the avenue shone just for her against a dense black background. There was still a glow in the sky on the horizon. It didn't matter that they had said it as a joke, which was the only plausible explanation. Just having said it was enough, whatever had been their intention. To have said it was irreversible. Just like that, and everything else was left behind. That meant the two punks had been left behind once and for all, like a sign read and understood so well that the entire world was its meaning.

But in reality they had not been left behind. Marcia had not gone twenty metres, and was still within the radius of The Cure's music, when they caught up with her.

'Wait a bit, are you in such a hurry?'

'Eh?'

'Are you deaf or just plain dumb?'

Marcia swallowed hard. She had come to a stop. She turned round halfway, and they were face-to-face. Just as before, the one who talked was in front, the other a step further back, to one side. They both looked very serious.

'Did I annoy you? Was there something wrong with what I said?'

'Of course!'

'Don't be such an old maid.'

'Get lost, will you? Leave me in peace.'

'Sorry. If you're angry, I'm sorry.' She paused. 'What happened? Did I scare you?'

'Me? Why?'

The stranger shrugged and said:

'If you want me to get lost, I will.'

It was Marcia's turn to shrug her shoulders. Of course she didn't want to offend anyone. But why was she to blame?

'Did you think it was a joke?'

The question was so accurate she felt in some way duty-bound to respond. Otherwise she would have walked on at once. A lot of things had happened during their previous dialogue. What had emerged most clearly was that it wasn't exactly a joke.

'That was a possibility,' she said. 'But I don't think so now.'

'If some guy had said that to you, would you have thought it? That it was a joke?'

'A bit less.' She said this without thinking, but it was true.

The girl pulled a face. 'Don't you believe in love?'

'In love, yes.'

'So what did I say?'

'It doesn't matter. Ciao.'

She took a step.

'Wait a moment. What's your name?'

'Marcia.'

The punk stared at her with that serious, neutral expression of hers. It was a heavy silence, although she could never have said what made it so heavy. At any rate, it was one of those silences that make you wait. It didn't even occur to her to walk away. She wouldn't have been able to anyway, because the silence lasted only a few seconds.

'What a lovely name. Listen to me, Marcia: what I told you is true. Love at first sight. It's *completely true*. Everything you might think . . . is *true*.'

'What's your name?'

'Mao.'

'Mao? You're crazy.'

23

'Why?'

'Just because.'

'No, tell me why.'

'I can't explain.'

'Do you believe in love between women?'

'If I'm honest, no I don't.'

'But hang on, Marcia, I don't mean platonic love.'

'Yes, I realised that.'

'And you don't believe in it?'

'But why did this have to happen to me?'

'You know why.'

Marcia looked at her, eyes wide with astonishment.

'Because you are you,' Mao explained. 'Because you're the one I love.'

Impossible to hold a rational conversation with her. Was the other one the same? Somehow Mao could read her mind, or possibly her gaze, and she made a brief introduction:

'She's called Lenin. We're lovers.'

The other punk nodded.

'But don't get me wrong, Marcia. We're not a couple. We're free. Like you. When I saw you on that corner, I fell in love. The same could have happened to her, and I would understand.'

'OK, that's fine,' said Marcia. 'It's not my thing.

I'm really sorry. Bye. Will you leave me in peace now? People are waiting for me.'

'Don't lie! Give me time. Don't you like sex? Don't you do it to . . . ?'

'How do you expect me to talk about something like that with a stranger in the street? I'm not interested in sex without love.'

'You misunderstood me, Marcia. Don't talk about sex, because that has nothing to do with it. What I want is to go to bed with you, kiss you on the mouth, suck those fat tits of yours, hug you like a doll . . . '

Marcia turned pale. She decided to turn round and head off without another word, but was afraid they might make a scene.

'I'm not a lesbian.'

'Nor am I.'

A pause.

'Look: I want to go . . . '

Her voice sounded oddly strangulated. Mao must have thought she was about to burst into tears, because her attitude and tone of voice changed abruptly.

'Don't be such a drama queen. We're not going to eat you. I'd never do anything to hurt you. Because I love you. That's what I'm trying to get you to understand. I love you.'

'Why do you say that?' asked Marcia in a whisper.

'Because it's true.'

'Anybody else would have told you to get lost.'

'But not you.'

'Because I'm stupid. Excuse me, I want to go.'

'Do you have a boyfriend?'

What a ridiculous question, at this point in the proceedings!

'No.'

'You see? Anybody else would have said yes, he's a weightlifter and he's waiting for me on the next corner. But you told me the truth.'

'What does that prove? That I'm even stupider than I thought, and I don't know how to get rid of the pair of you.'

'Listen, Marcia, does it upset you that Lenin is here? Do you want her to leave so the two of us can talk on our own?'

'No! No, I'm the one who wants to leave.' She thought for a moment: 'Aren't you ashamed of treating your friend like that, your "lover", as you call her?'

'I'd do the same for her, and a lot more. An awful lot more. Don't get it wrong, Marcia, we're not a couple of sluts.'

'Did you make a bet?' Marcia looked in the direction they had come from. The possibility had just occurred to her. But nobody was watching them.

'Don't talk crap. I'm not such an arsehole.'

Marcia gave her that. She didn't know why, but she conceded it.

'OK . . . ' she said with a smile. The conversation had gone on long enough. 'Pleasure meeting you . . . '

'Allow me just one more question, Marcia. I've already asked lots, so one more won't hurt. Do you know what love is?'

'I think so.'

'Have you ever been in love?'

'No.'

'Can I ask you a more intimate question?'

'No, but thanks for asking. In the end, you're not that much of a brute, are you? It's like you weren't a real punk.'

'Would you like it if all three of us went to bed together?' asked Lenin. This was the first thing she had said. Her voice was soft and pleasant.

'You too?' said Marcia despairingly.

The two punks talked amongst themselves.

'Do you like her?' asked Mao.

'I didn't at first, but I do a bit more now.'

'She's so different from us.'

'I do like her now, I could fall in love with her.'

Marcia wasn't upset by this exchange; on the contrary, it made her feel almost at ease for the first time. Mao turned resolutely towards her, as though something important had taken place.

'Lenin is good, she's passionate, she's made me come a lot. I always listen to her because she's intelligent, much more than I am. Did you hear what she said? She confirmed me in my opinion. It's settled. It was before anyway, but I wasn't completely certain. What can I do to convince you?'

This was a question that called for a reply, a concrete reply. Marcia thought about it.

'Let me go.'

'No. I want the opposite. I want you to say yes, to throw yourself into my arms. But this isn't getting us anywhere. Would you like the three of us just to talk, about anything, not love, like friends? What do girls like you talk about? Do you want us to go window-shopping? Don't say someone is waiting for you, because it's not true. I'm not going to try to pick you up. You can't deny us a bit of your time.'

'What for?'

'Just because; to add something to life, to get to know people . . . '

'No, I mean what would *you* do it for?'

'I won't lie: I'm doing it to gain time, because I love you and I want to fuck you. But that can wait.'

Marcia said nothing.

'What's your problem?' asked Mao.

All of a sudden Marcia felt free, almost happy.

'Well . . . ' she said hesitantly. 'I've always wanted to get to know a punk, but I've never had the opportunity.'

'Good. At last you're being reasonable.'

'But don't get your hopes up.'

'I'll worry about that.'

'One more thing: I want you to promise me that if at the end I say goodbye and leave, which is what I'm going to do, you two won't follow me and kick up a fuss. More than that: I want you to promise that if right now I say goodbye and leave, you won't move an inch.'

'Listen, Marcia, it would be very easy to promise you that or anything else. But I won't. I won't kick up a fuss, or do anything bad to you, *anything*, I promise, but I'm not going to let you go. Would it be love if I promised you that? It's for your own good. Besides, you yourself say you wanted to get to know punks. Are you going to get another opportunity?' When she saw Marcia's impatient reaction, she raised her hand to calm her, and added: 'Let's go back to what we agreed, and talk about something else.'

'Let's go to Pumper,' said Lenin.

She set off across the street right there, in the middle of the block, striding between the cars and dragging the other two after her. Marcia glanced at Mao out of the corner of her eye: she seemed distracted, as if she was thinking of something else. She admired her for never once smiling; she herself was always smiling because she was nervous, and she hated the habit.

Inside, the Pumper Nic was a blaze of white neon light, and the heating was on full blast. The three of them entered together, or rather in a straggling line, with Mao bringing up the rear. Were they surrounding her in case she tried to escape? No, that couldn't be it. They went in like three friends: two of one kind, the third another sort. Marcia felt calm and almost happy. Putting an end to the scene outside was a relief. It was as if they were entering another more normal and predictable stage. They attracted stares from all the few customers there; people were always curious about punks. Since the other two took the lead, Marcia was able to study them just as the others were doing. Dressed in black from head to foot, with thin black jeans, Mao had on a man's black jacket over a T-shirt made of some strange heavy cloth, and black trainers. Lenin was wearing a worn leather jacket and boots without laces, all in black as well. They both had lots of ugly metal necklaces and pins round their necks, and chains round their waists and wrists. Their hair was half shaved and half worn in long strands dyed red, brick-red and purple. Confrontational, taking on the world, dangerous (or so they would like to think). What impression would they make on this ultra-normal public of youngsters, adults and children busy eating their hamburgers and drinking their soft drinks? Would they feel invaded, threatened? Marcia could not avoid the childish satisfaction of thinking they were jealous of her for being with them, for having access to their strange way of being and thinking. Perhaps they would think they were childhood friends who had taken different paths in life, and had got together to exchange experiences. Or maybe they thought (after all, it was more logical) that she was a punk too, except that her hair and clothes were conventional. She quickened her pace to catch up with the others: she didn't want anyone making a mistake and thinking it was only a coincidence she had come in with them. An assistant was polishing the floor; they stepped on the cable of his machine as if it wasn't there. Marcia didn't tread on it; to avoid it seemed so natural to her that her companions' strange attitude became almost supernatural. Unless they were putting it on, but it didn't seem like it.

There was a long corridor with tables that led from the first room to another one at the back, where a children's birthday party was being held. Her guides in black did not go very far down it, but sat at a big table before the halfway point. Fortunately the ones on either side were empty. There wasn't much risk of them being heard anyway because of the music and the din from the children at the party. What was more disturbing was their automatic behaviour: Mao leaned against the wall and put her feet up on the chair. She was on her own on one side, because Marcia had sat down opposite her, next to Lenin; it seemed to be the rule that she had to turn to talk to her, and she didn't question it. The first thing Marcia said as they were sitting down was an instinctive reaction:

'You have to order up at the counter.'

'What the fuck do I care?'

Marcia realised she had gone too far in persuading herself that things were more normal now. Going into the Pumper Nic in a group, like the local schoolgirls did, had led her to believe they were going to behave like everyone else, even if they were only using this as a place to explain things. But it wasn't going to be like that. They had no intention of ordering anything, and that was only to be expected. Punks didn't do fast food. She recalled having seen them drinking straight from big bottles of beer in the doorways.

'We'll get thrown out if we don't have something,' she said.

'I'd like to see them dare say a single word to me,' said Mao, peering round her with a look of profound scorn.

'We said there'd be no scenes.'

The two punks looked at her with neutral, serious expressions. That expression, which expressed nothing, was one of pure violence. They were violence. There was no escaping the fact. She wasn't going to emerge scot-free from her audience with the punks, as she had absent-mindedly assumed. This was not the same as any other strange specimen in society, which could be dealt with by finding the proper setting in which to examine it. Because they themselves were the setting. She resigned herself to it: she had never set foot in this Pumper before, and had no problem in never coming back if they were thrown out.

But the so-called Mao had an idea, and didn't keep it to herself:

'Do you want something, Marcia? A Coke, a beer?'

This had its funny side. She was asking her if she 'could buy her a drink', and that was one of the classic chat-up lines.

'Do you want to tell us what the fuck you're laughing at, *Marcia*?'

'I remembered a joke I heard from Porcel on TV the other night. In the sketch where he's a newspaper seller. An old Spanish guy comes up and tells him he was once at the San Fermín fiesta in Pamplona. They let the bulls loose, and he started running. He was running, with the bull right behind him . . . him in front, the bull behind . . . When they came to a corner, the King was going by. So he, like the good subject he was, bowed low before him . . . and the bull . . . So Porcel asks him: Just like that? Without even asking him for a drink first?'

She burst out laughing, but the others didn't join in. They didn't even smile.

'Who is Porcel?' asked Lenin.

'You don't know Fatty Porcel?'

'He's a guy on TV,' Mao explained to Lenin.

'And is he fat? His name must mean "porker".'

'Just out of curiosity,' said Marcia, 'did you get the joke?'

'Yes,' said Mao. 'The bull stuck a horn up his arse. If that's a joke . . . '

'It was funny because of the way he said it, the improvisation. I don't know how to tell jokes.'

Mao sighed and straightened up opposite her, as if she were resigned to saying something completely banal:

'You told it very well. But it's difficult for something like that to be funny, Marcia. You must tell yourself those jokes very well, you're always laughing.'

'I laugh because I'm nervous, not because something's funny. Not just now: always. I admire people who can stay serious whenever dreadful things happen to them.'

'That's paradoxical. You're very intelligent, Marcia. It's good to talk to an intelligent person for a change.'

'You don't have intelligent friends?'

'I don't have friends.'

'Nor do I,' said Lenin.

Marcia preferred to change tack:

'Do you really not watch TV?'

Neither of them deigned to reply. Mao had slumped back in her chair. Where was the supervisor who would come to tell her to take her feet off the chair, or to throw them out straight away if they weren't going to have anything? Marcia was sitting with her back to the counter, and so couldn't see the preparations that must be under way to expel them.

'Whatever,' said Mao. 'We couldn't buy you anything because we have no dough.'

'I do. But I don't know if it's enough to buy beer or hamburgers. It's expensive here . . . '

She paused when she realised her words had fallen flat. A silence followed.

'Thanks, *Marcia,* don't worry about it.'

'Why do you repeat my name the whole time?'

'Because I like it. I like it more than I could explain. Of the stupid names they give women it's the only one I like, and I've only just discovered it now.'

'You don't like any names?' Marcia asked her, trying to head off the fresh declaration of love she could sense coming.

'None. They're all ridiculous.'

'What are you called? Really, I mean.'

'Nothing. Mao. Lenin.'

'And you think ordinary names are ridiculous! I'd say you're called . . . Amalia . . . and Elena. How strange, they're my favourites. And I've just discovered that too.'

'That's not what we're called,' said Lenin-Elena, as if Marcia had really tried to guess. But Mao-Amalia suddenly sprang back to life and silenced her from the far side of the table.

'Would you like us to be called Amalia and Elena? Because if that's the case, consider it done. It's not in the least important to us.'

'Is that so? Do you change names every day, just like that? To the name that the person you're with prefers?'

'No. In that case we would choose the name that "person", as you call them, hates most.'

It was Lenin who had spoken, and she did so with a touch of irony that was refreshing against the background of deadly seriousness they gave every-thing. And when Mao spoke again, it was just as seriously:

'Which doesn't mean we can't change names as often as we damn well like. But I'm telling you, Marcia, that from tomorrow on the two of us, Lenin and I, we're going to call ourselves "Marcia". What do you think?'

'Why from tomorrow on?' asked Marcia.

'Because tomorrow will be an important date in our lives,' she replied cryptically.

They fell silent again for a moment. Mao was staring at her. Marcia looked away, but not before she noted something very odd, which she could not define there and then. The silence dragged on, as if the three of them had thought the same thing and none of them knew what it was. Eventually Mao, like someone carrying out a painful obligation, but in a friendly way, addressed Marcia:

'What did you want to know about us?'

Marcia had no time even to begin to think what questions she wanted to ask, because at that moment the Pumper supervisor appeared at their table. She had dyed blonde hair, and was wearing a white blouse and grey miniskirt.

'If you're not going to have anything, you can't stay.'

Marcia was about to tell her that in fact she was going to order an ice cream (the idea occurred to her at that very instant), but her jaw dropped before she could emit a sound because Mao got in before her:

'Go fuck yourself.'

The supervisor looked stunned, although on second thoughts, what else could she have expected? She seemed a lively sort: she was very attractive, about twenty-five years old. The kind of woman who wouldn't be pushed around, Marcia decided.

'What?'

'Fuck off and leave us in peace. We need to talk.'

'Start by taking your foot off the chair.'

Mao responded by removing both feet and scraping them noisily. 'That all right? Now leave us in peace. Move.'

The supervisor turned on her heel and walked away. Marcia was astounded. She couldn't help admiring the punks. In theory, she was not unaware that other people could be treated that way; but in practice she had never tried it, and it wasn't something she planned to do. She told herself that when it came to it, reality was more theoretical than thought.

When she came out of this momentary reflection, it was as if the nature of Pumper had changed.

It wasn't the first time she had felt this since the two girls had stopped her on the far pavement, less than quarter of an hour earlier: the world had been transformed time and again. It seemed like a permanent feature of the effect they had on it. It would be logical to presume that this effect would wear off the longer it went on; no one is an everlasting box of surprises, and despite the strangeness of the two punks, she could make out a shallow depth to them: the vulgarity of two lost girls playing a role. Once the play was over there would be nothing left, no secret, they would be as boring as a chemistry class . . . And yet at the same time she could imagine the opposite, even though as yet she didn't know why: maybe the world, once it has been transformed once, can no longer stop changing.

'Wait for me a minute,' she said, getting up. 'I'm going to ask for an ice cream. That way they won't bother us any more.'

'If that's the reason, don't worry,' said Mao. 'No one's going to bother you. We'll make sure of that.'

'But I *want* an ice cream,' said Marcia, only half lying. 'Don't you want one?'

'No.'

She went to the front counter. She had to wait a while for the assistant to serve several coffees and teas with slices of cake. She was by the door, and nothing would have been easier than to leave, run to the corner, or catch a bus . . . Back at the table, neither of them was looking in her direction. But she didn't want to escape. Or rather, she did want to, but not until she had found out more about them. So she waited her turn patiently, ordered an ice cream with a chocolate topping, and came back with it on a tray. All at once she really felt like having one. An ice cream in winter accentuated things; and a half-truth that became the complete truth accentuated them still further. The supervisor who had threatened them passed by, in such a busy rush she didn't even look at them. It was as though everybody was thinking about something else, and doubtless they were. Wasn't it true that after a certain length of time everybody did think about something else? Added to the ice cream, the idea comforted her. She sat back down with her friends and tasted it.

'Delicious,' she said.

The other two looked at her absent-mindedly, as though from a long way off. Were they thinking of something else too? Had they forgotten their intentions? Marcia picked at the chocolate topping rather anxiously, but didn't have to wait long for things to get back on track.

'What did you want to ask us, Marcia?' Mao reminded her.

'To be honest, nothing in particular. Besides, I don't think you can give me answers. In general I believe questions and answers aren't the best way to find out about things.'

'What do you mean?'

'In abstract terms, I'd like to know what punks think, why they become punks; all that. But at the same time I ask myself: why do I want to know that, what does it matter to me?'

It was all very logical, very rational, and she could have carried on a long time in that vein, until she had turned the whole situation into a 'Marcian' one. Some hope! Mao made sure to burst that balloon straight away.

'How fuckin' stupid you are, Marcia.'

'Why?' And then, correcting herself at once (correcting herself because Mao was incorrigible). 'Yes, I am stupid. You're right. I should become a punk if I want to know what it means, and to know why I want to know.'

'No.' Mao interrupted her with a sarcastic, humourless little laugh. 'You're completely wrong. You're far more stupid than even you imagine. We're not "punks".'

'What are you, then?'

'You would never understand.'

'Besides,' Lenin interrupted her, in her less abrupt manner, 'don't you think it's absurd to think *you* could become a punk? Have you looked at yourself in the mirror?'

'Are you saying that because I'm . . . overweight?' asked Marcia, who was hurt and whose eyes showed it despite herself.

Lenin seemed almost about to smile: 'Quite the opposite . . . '

'Quite the opposite,' Mao repeated fervently. 'How can you not see it?'

She paused for an instant, and Marcia's astonishment floated in the air.

'You were right,' Lenin said finally to her friend. 'She's incredibly stupid.'

Marcia ate a spoonful of ice cream. She felt excused to try another topic.

'What do you mean you're not punks?' The only response was a click of the tongue from Mao. 'For example, don't you like The Cure?'

Like two sphinxes.

Lenin deigned to ask: 'What's that?'

'The English group, the musicians. *I* like them. Robert Smith is a genius.'

'Never heard them.'

'He's that cretin who wears lipstick and make-up. I saw him on the cover of a magazine.'

'What an arsehole.'

'But it's theatre,' stammered Marcia, 'it's . . . provocation, that's all. I don't think he wears make-up because he likes it. The look is part of the philosophy he represents . . . '

'He's still an arsehole.'

'Do you prefer heavy metal?'

'We don't prefer anything, Marcia.'

'You don't like music?'

'Music is idiotic.'

'Freddie Mercury is idiotic?'

'Of course.'

'What nihilists you are. I can't believe you really think that.'

Mao's eyes narrowed and she said nothing. Marcia returned to the charge:

'What do you like, then?'

Mao's eyes narrowed still further (they were almost completely shut by now) and still said nothing. Lenin sighed and said:

'The answer you're expecting is "nothing". But we're not going to say "nothing". You're going to have to go on asking questions, although you may think they won't get you anywhere.'

'I give up.'

'Congratulations,' said Mao. She relaxed and opened her eyes to look around her. 'What a dump this is. Do you know something, Marcia? In places like this where there are waitresses who have to be single to get a job, there's always at least one who's pregnant. So there's always at least one tragedy in the offing.'

'They're feminists,' thought Marcia whilst Mao was saying this. It was a small, automatic conclusion that rather disappointed her. She looked up from her ice cream and saw that one of the uniformed girls sweeping up was staring at them. She was studying them with great curiosity, and not trying to hide it. She was almost as young as they were, short, fair-haired and plump, with the ruddy complexion of a European peasant girl. Marcia felt strangely uneasy under her scrutiny. Because she looked extraordinarily like her: they were exactly the same type. She felt an irrational urge to hide her from her two friends. The waitress diminished her own value; Mao and Lenin might see she wasn't the only one cut from that cloth. But the punks' minds were elsewhere. They had seen her and not noticed the likeness (there wasn't in fact a like-ness, it was more the fact of belonging to the same type). Mao said to her:

'Now you'll see,' and called the girl over. She came at once. 'I said I'd bring . . . a cardie and some bootees to a girl who works here and is pregnant,' she told her, 'but I can't remember her name. Which one is it?'

'Pregnant?'

'Yes. Are you deaf, you fat cow?'

'It's Matilde who's pregnant.'

'So?'

'A tall, dark girl.'

'That's the one,' Mao lied.

'She's on the morning shift. She's already left. We have three shifts, in rotation . . . '

'What the fuck is that to me? Thanks. Ciao.'

'Do you want to leave the things for her?'

'And have them stolen? No. On your way. Give me room to breathe.'

The waitress would gladly have continued the conversation. She didn't seem in the least bit offended by Mao's rudeness.

'How did you meet her?'

'What fuckin' business is that of yours? Get lost; we have to talk.'

'OK. Don't get mad. It was you who asked me a question.'

'What's your name?' Lenin asked.

'Liliana.'

'How much do you make?'

'The minimum wage.'

'How stupid you lot are,' said Mao. 'I don't under-stand why you work.'

'I work to help out my family. And I study.'

'What?'

'Medicine.'

'Don't make me laugh. Carry on sweeping, doctor,' said Mao.

'I have to finish secondary school.'

'Of course. And primary school as well.'

'No, I finished primary. I'm in the third year of secondary. When I finish here I go to evening classes. I make sacrifices to get on. The problem with this country is that no one wants to work.'

Mao straightened in her seat and glared directly at Liliana.

'You've no idea how sick you make me feel. Get lost, before I hit you.'

'Why would you do that? Besides, I'd fight back. I've got a strong character.'

She said all this with the shyness of a sleepwalker. She seemed half-witted, half simple. There was one way she was different to Marcia: she didn't smile. She went off still sweeping the floor, but as if to say: I'll be right back.

'What a dummy,' said Lenin.

'Why?' said Marcia. 'There must be a lot like her. Working and studying . . . We should have asked her if she had a boyfriend.'

'Didn't you see she's deformed? Who's going to want to fuck a monster like that!'

Marcia's surprise only grew. From surprise she went to surprise within surprise. Not only had Liliana not seemed deformed to her (on the contrary, she had been struck by her self-assured normality, often found in dim-witted people) and had seen her as her own double. Marcia was typically young in that she could only see love as a question of general types; you fell in love with a set of characteristics that you found in a certain individual, but which could also exist in somebody else. You only had to find the one possessing them. For the young, that is love, it is why they young are so restless, so sociable, always searching; because love can be anywhere, everywhere; for them, the whole world is love.

But if the punks had not fallen in love with the type she represented . . . what was it, then? Where was the key? Mao had told her she had been waiting for her, that she had only to see her to know she loved her. That meant she knew what she was like, what she ought to be. But now that didn't seem to be the case.

Still confused by all this, she came to Liliana's defence.

'You're wrong,' she told Mao. 'She's not deformed, or ugly, and I bet she does have a boyfriend. No, don't call her over,' she said, seeing Mao stirring. 'It doesn't matter what she might say. Tell me the truth: isn't she pretty in her own way? She's childish, and a bit slow, but there are dozens of boys who like that sort. She could make you feel you want to protect her, for example . . . '

'She makes me feel I want to crush her like an insect.'

'Can't you see? There are people who get married for less than that.' She paused, then took a risk: 'In fact, that's my only hope of not turning into an old maid. Didn't you notice that she's the same kind as me?'

The look Mao gave her froze her blood. She had the ghastly feeling she had been reading her mind all this time. More than that: she had deliberately been leading her on, all this had been a sadistic manoeuvre. She quickly changed subjects.

'Why were you so aggressive? Why did you treat her so badly, when she seemed so sweet?'

'No one is sweet deep down,' said Lenin. (Her companion seemed to reserve herself for more important declarations.)

'That's a preconception. Nobody is going to be sweet towards *you* if you think and act the way you do. You have to be more optimistic.'

'Don't talk crap,' said Mao, who had apparently decided that the time for important declarations had arrived. 'You're play-acting. Imitating that poor dummy. "I make sacrifices . . . " Her sort need to be destroyed.'

'Why?'

'Because she suffers. So that she won't suffer any more.'

'But she doesn't suffer. She wants to be a doctor, to be happy. She's . . . innocent. She seemed very nice and sweet to me. I'd help her if I could, rather than insult her like you did. She thinks everyone is good deep down, and probably still thinks so, despite the way you two treated her.'

'She can think what she likes. But I'm sure she'd plunge a knife in my back at the first opportunity.'

'No, I don't think so.'

'If she dared to, she would. The only help I'd be happy to give her is to teach her how to stab people in the back. That would be more useful to her than becoming a doctor.'

'I think I understand something now,' said Marcia. 'What you want is for evil to rule in this world. You want to destroy innocence.'

'Don't talk nonsense.'

'We don't want anything,' said Lenin.

'Nothing?'

'Nothing like that. It's useless.'

Useless? That gave Marcia a hint:

'Does that mean there are other things, other actions, that are useful? What are they?'

'You really get my goat with all your blah-blah,' said Mao. 'That's a good example of uselessness.'

'So what is useful then? What's the point of living? Tell me, please.'

'You're playing at being Liliana. I won't talk to you until you are yourself again.'

This was true, up to a point. Except that Marcia didn't think she could get anywhere (and not only on this occasion, but always) if she didn't swap roles, adopt other characters. Otherwise she finished up in dead ends, fell into the abyss, was paralysed with fear. At that moment it occurred to her that perhaps this fear was something she had to confront, to accept. That could be the lesson of this punk nihilism. But she didn't believe it; on the one hand, her two companions would deny that they had any lesson to give her; on the other, they themselves, in the disguises they had adopted, were a rebuttal of that morality, despite the fact that it wasn't so ridiculous, given the atmosphere in which they moved, where all values were changing.

'All right,' she said. 'But before I give up my role as Liliana, there's something I want to say: I identify with her through innocence. I couldn't care less what nonsense she might talk, nor the pity she might inspire: she is innocent, and I'd like to be just as innocent as her. I probably am. You say nobody would fuck her. You're completely wrong, but that doesn't matter. Let's say she is a virgin . . . like me.' She paused: if this wasn't the abyss, it was something very like it. Neither of the others said anything. 'When you two intercepted me, I was walking along in a world where seduction was very discreet, very invisible. Everything that was being said and was going on in the street was a sign of seduction, because the world seduces a virgin, but nothing was aimed specifically at me. Then you two appeared, with your abrupt Wannafuck? It was as if innocence became personified, not exactly in you or in me, but in the situation, in the words (I can't explain it). Before then, the world was talking, but saying nothing. Afterwards, when you said that, innocence removed her mask. Now look at Liliana. She represents the same thing, and sometimes I think there's no such thing as coincidence. She talks of her life as if it were natural to do so. It's another way of speaking, even more violent than yours, if you like. At first I thought she put me in the shade, but in fact it's you two she diminishes. Although in the end it's the same innocence, and that innocence is the only thing I can understand.'

'That means you don't understand a thing,' Mao interrupted her with characteristic distant disdain. 'There's nothing more to say.'

'I don't understand why you refuse to discuss these things!'

'You will, I promise you. Have you finished?'

'Yes.'

'I'm glad. Let's talk about something else.'

They fell silent for a moment. The Pumper had started to fill up, and this reassured Marcia, because they were more easily hidden in the crowd. But if all the tables became occupied, which seemed likely to happen soon, they would come and throw the three of them out. They had finished the ice cream. As if it were a charm to prevent them from being interrupted, Marcia quickly raised another question she thought might lead somewhere:

'Earlier today, opposite here, were you with someone?'

'No. I already told you, we were on our own.'

'There were so many people . . . '

'We'd mixed with those stupid kids to see if we could pick somebody up, but we didn't know anyone and didn't have time to choose because then you appeared . . . '

This information offered a few interesting elements, but seemed deliberately to ensure that they were of the kind Marcia preferred not to pursue. So she continued along the same line she had already taken.

'Do you belong to some group or other?'

'What does that mean?'

'I mean some group of punks.'

'No,' said Mao, venomously emphasising every word she said: 'We're not part of any carnival band.'

'I didn't mean it badly. People always like to associate with others who share their ideas, their tastes, their way of being.'

'Like you and Liliana, for example? Do you belong to a group of innocents?'

'Don't try to twist what I'm saying. And don't pretend not to understand. Here and everywhere else in the world punks get together and support each other in their rejection of society.'

'Bravo for your erudition. The answer is no.'

'But you do know other punks?'

She was proud of her own question. She should have asked it right at the start. It was a perfect lure. It was as though someone had asked them if they knew other human beings. If they denied it, which is obviously what they wanted to do, that would show their bad faith. She had no idea what good that would do her, but at least she would have an answer.

Mao's eyes narrowed once more. She was too intelligent not to spot how great the danger was. But she wouldn't let herself be forced into anything. Ever.

'Why is that important?' she said. 'Why are you always trying to get us to talk about what we're not interested in?'

'We made a pact. We made an agreement.'

'All right. What was your question?'

Marcia said implacably:

'If you know other punks.'

Mao, to Lenin:

'Do you know any?'

'There's Sergio Vicio.'

'Oh yes, of course, Sergio ... ' She turned to Marcia. 'He's an acquaintance of ours. We haven't seen him for ages, but he's an excellent example. Shame we don't have a photo of him. He was the bass guitarist in a band; he was always high, and was a great kid. He still must be, though he's a bit crazy, out of it. When he talks, which isn't very often, you can't understand a word. Something extraordinary happened to him once. A very rich woman went to a party, and amongst other things she was wearing a pair of earrings that had four emeralds as big as saucers in each of them. All of a sudden she realised one was missing; and even though they turned over all the sofas and carpets, they couldn't find it. Since it cost millions, and rich women are very concerned about their possessions, which always cost millions, there was a huge scandal, which even got into the papers. All the guests agreed to allow themselves to be searched on the way out, apart from the Paraguayan ambassador, who refused and wasn't frisked. Of course, that made him the prime suspect. The foreign ministry got involved, and the ambassador was recalled to his country and lost his post. A year later, the same lady went to a party at Palladium. Imagine her surprise when on the dance floor she spotted Sergio Vicio, with the four emeralds dangling from one ear. Her bodyguards went for him at once, and brought him back by the scruff of his neck. She was with a colonel, the Interior Minister, Pirker, and Mitterrand's wife. They brought another chair and made Sergio Vicio sit down. As they had been talking in French at the table, the lady in question asked him if he spoke the language. Sergio said he did. "Some time ago," she told him, "I lost an earring that was identical to yours. I wonder if it's the same one?"

Sergio looked at her, but couldn't see (or hear) her. He had been dancing for three or four hours non-stop, something he often does because he loves to dance, and when the movement ended all of a sudden he had a problem with his blood pressure. This was the first time it had happened to him, because he always instinctively stopped dancing gradually, and then went out to walk until dawn. The effect of being hauled off the dance floor left him blind: everything was covered with little red dots and he couldn't see a thing. It's called "orthostatic hypotension", but he didn't know that. Other symptoms accompanying the vision loss are nausea, which he didn't get because he hadn't had a bite to eat in two or three days, and vertigo, which he was used to because of all the dope he smoked, and which, far from upsetting or alarming him, kept him amused during all the rest of the scene, which he spent rocking himself in cosmic space. The lady, a light-fingered expert, made the earring disappear from his ear as if it was a magic trick. Now at the party being held there that night, which was in honour of a French orchestra visiting Argentina, Palladium was inaugurating a system of quartz strobe lights, the cutting edge of technology. And they switched them on at that very moment. At the table they were so taken up with Sergio Vicio they didn't hear the announcement.

When the lady had taken the earring from his ear, she held it up by the little hook for all of them to see and began to say: "These emeralds . . . " She didn't manage to get any further, because as the new lights hit the stones they made them completely transparent like the purest crystal. There was no trace of green in them. Her jaw dropped. "Emeralds?" said Mitterrand's wife. "But they're diamonds. And of the first water! I've never seen anything like them." "What do you mean, diamonds?" said Pirker. "Where would this layabout get something like that? They're bits of glass from some granny's chandelier, tied together with wire." Struck dumb, their owner was gasping like an axolotl. And at that moment, the first bars of *Pierrot Lunaire* could be heard. No less a personage than Pierre Boulez was onstage, with the fantastic Helga Pilarczyk as soprano. The guests at the table transferred their attention to the music. No emerald turned into a diamond could compare with the moonlit notes of this masterpiece. The most basic elegance dictated the supremacy of music over gems. Moving like a robot, the lady copied her previous gesture in reverse, and fixed the earring back on Sergio Vicio's earlobe, then watched in anguished silence as the bodyguards, misinterpreting what was going on, lifted him up and deposited him back on the dance floor. He started dancing again, regardless of the music, until he got his sight back and left to go for a walk, still on automatic pilot. And she never saw her emeralds again.'

Silence.

Marcia couldn't believe it. This was the first time in her life that she had heard a well-told story, and it had seemed to her sublime, an experience that made up for all the fears this meeting had caused.

'It's . . . marvellous,' she stammered. 'I know I ought to thank you, but I can't find the words. You've surprised me far more than I could say . . . While you were talking I felt transported. It was as if I could see everything . . . '

Mao waved her hand dismissively. This was such a new experience for Marcia that she couldn't help thinking of the rules of etiquette there must be in such cases. She had to discover them all on her own, as they went along. To start with, she grasped that it was not done to go on praising the form; such praise had to be transmitted implicitly in her comments on the content. But she was so dazzled that content and form became intertwined; whatever she might say about the former would inevitably be transferred to the latter. The most practical things – and what came most naturally to her – were questions, doubts. What happened next to Sergio Vicio? And the earring? How had he got in to that party at Palladium? Had the two of them ever been there? Marcia of course had never set foot in the famous nightspot. Probably the punks were allowed in free, even on the most important occasions, to add some local colour, as part of the decor. To her, Palladium had all the hallmarks of somewhere from a dream, and it was no surprise to her that all those famous, important people were there . . . It was almost another world, but one linked to this one through the fantastic aspect of the tale . . . Could it be that her friends had been in Palladium *that night*? How had they heard about what had happened? That was what was important, and to a certain extent that was what the story of the earring was about . . .

She began asking them questions, which they seemed to find inopportune. Who were the musicians they had mentioned? The only one that sounded well-known to her was the one called Pierrot. She thought she remembered he had played with Tom Verlaine in Television. Mao's art as a narrator had transported her from the plebeian neon lighting of the Pumper to the shadows of this dream, shot through with that lunar glow. She even thought she had heard a song she had never heard before, something that, almost inconceivably, was even better than The Cure and the Rolling Stones . . .

None of her questions got an answer because a second supervisor had appeared at their table. This one was formidable, threatening, and demanded to be taken into account. She was exactly the sort of person who had to be taken into account. Especially as she was the spitting image of the first supervisor, with each of her features intensified: she was taller, her hair even more dyed; her miniskirt even shorter. She was prettier, sterner, more determined. Whereas the other one seemed like someone who wouldn't allow herself to be pushed around (that must be a requisite for the job), this one was the model of a strong character, of energetic initiative.

'Get out.'

Her voice left no room for doubt. Marcia would have happily got up and left. She glanced at Mao, who slowly raised her eyes towards the intruder like a cobra uncoiling. Here was a worthy opponent. The Liliana phase was over. The establishment had kept its heavy artillery for the end.

'What's wrong with you?'

'You have to leave.'

'What?' It really was as if Mao were coming out of a dream. 'What . . . ? And who are you?'

'The super . . . '

All at once Lenin had an open flick knife in her hand. The blade was twenty centimetres long, and sharp as a razor. Marcia blenched. Lenin was sitting on the same side as her, next to the wall. If there was an attack, she was blocking her exit. But it didn't seem as if things would get that far. Mao glanced at her friend and said:

'Put that away, there's no need for it.'

'Do you want me to call the police?' said the supervisor, making to move away.

Mao took her time replying:

'You've got such a fucking ugly bitch's face.'

'Do you want me to call the police?'

'Yes, please. Go on, call them.'

All this, noted Marcia, was said in a paroxysm of violence that revealed a new dimension to the punks . . . and also, yet again, to the world. They faced each other like two powerful beasts, both of them sure of their own strength, and even of the balance of power between them, at an excessive level. In confrontations of this sort, victory went to whoever possessed a secret weapon, and it was obvious that in this case it was Mao who had it.

'You were threatening one of the girls . . . ' said the supervisor.

'Which girl? Liliana? But she's a friend of ours.'

Slightly disconcerted, the supervisor looked over at Marcia, who nodded. That was a point in her favour, but it was a shame that Mao immediately threw it away:

'We're waiting for her to finish her shift to go and have a fuck. Do you have a problem with that?'

'Are you making fun of me, you piece of scum?'

'No, shithead. Liliana is a lezzie, and delighted to go to bed with us. Do you want to stop her?'

'I'm going to ask her right now.'

'You think she'd tell you the truth? If you do, you're not just a bitch, you're a cretin.'

'Liliana gets off at ten, and you're not going to spend hours here.'

'We're going to stay as long as we fuckin' well like. Ciao. Go call the cops.'

They stared each other out for a moment. The supervisor moved away, with a look on her face that said: I'll be right back. They all left with this same threat, but never returned.

When the tense moment had passed and she had recovered the power of speech, Marcia felt completely shocked.

'How could you be such a traitor! You put it all on to poor Liliana! That could cost her the job. I think her minutes are counted.'

'Why?'

'D'you think they will want a lesbian employee who makes dates with lovers who pull out flick knives?'

'It's all relative, Marcia. Maybe now they'll respect

her more. And if they throw her out, she'll find a better job: that's life. That means we've probably done her a favour without meaning to. She didn't seem to me particularly happy with what she's doing. The fact that she spoke to us shows that she is open to other possibilities.'

'Possibly,' said Marcia, not convinced. 'But anyway, I'm not happy about lying. That's always an insult. To me, truth is sacred.'

'Not to me.'

'Or me,' said Lenin.

'So much the worse for you. It devalues everything you've said . . . '

For the first time since they had come in, Mao showed genuine interest, as if Marcia had finally hit on a topic that was worth considering.

'Fine,' she said. 'So what?'

'What d'you mean, "So what?"'

'I mean, why is that important?'

'It's important because it is. It's what makes the difference between talking for its own sake and wanting to say something.'

Mao shook her head.

'Do you think anything we've said since we sat here is important?'

This was not a completely rhetorical question: she was expecting a reply.

'Yes,' said Marcia. 'It was important for me.'

'Well then, you're mistaken.'

'If that's what you think, why bother to speak at all?'

'If for nothing else, to make you understand that, Marcia: that none of it is important. That's it's all nothing, or the same as nothing.'

'And you told me you weren't nihilists!'

'We're not. *You* are the nihilist. Could you really spend your life talking crap, worried about the kind of things that happen here, in this hamburger microcosm? All this is accidental, nothing more than the springboard to launch us back to what is important. Which brings us back to our starting point. Are you satisfied now? Have you found out all you wanted to know about us? Can we get back to talking about the other?'

'I don't get you, Mao . . . ' There was a pleading note to her voice that was completely involuntary. But as she said the punk's name, Marcia once more felt the indefinable something was now closer to her awareness, but still outside it. The restaurant had become unreal, perhaps due to the constant coming and going of adolescents along the corridor, or the dazzling white lighting, or more probably because they had been sitting without moving for a while, which was something Marcia always detested. There was a mirror on the wall, which she looked at for the first time: she was pale, glassy-eyed. The faces of the other two looked veiled. 'I don't feel well. I think that ice cream disagreed with me. What time can it be?' Her question fell into an indifferent silence. 'Isn't the time important to you either? I guess not. Of course not. Why should it be? What gives you the right to decide what's important for me and what isn't? You don't know me, and I don't know you. Who are you? What do you want?'

'I've already told you that.'

What did they want? Who were they? Who was she? Everything was blurred in a corrosive mist. Marcia felt paralysed. If she moved, she would evaporate like a smoke ring. OK, so nothing was important. They were right after all. Some young boys went by, arguing loudly. Behind them was Liliana, with that swaying gait of hers. She glanced at the table as if this was the first time she had seen it, lifted the tray with her left hand and used her other hand to wipe it with a wet cloth, even though there was no need because they hadn't made it dirty. As she was doing so, she said:

'We get all kinds of weirdos in here.'

'Let's go,' said Mao, suddenly standing up.

Lenin imitated her, and since in order to get out she needed Marcia to get up, she took her arm and helped her stand. Mao took the other arm, and the two of them pointed her towards the door. Serious, inscrutable, still holding the tray, Liliana kept staring at them until they were outside.

The cold air revived Marcia. It was not that cold, but the heating inside the Pumper had been too high and she could feel the contrast, especially because she had not taken off her pullover. By the time they had taken a few steps, her discomfort had vanished . . . possibly because it had never really existed. She felt very lucid; her thoughts stirred and spread, even though there was still nothing to apply them to. This gave her a sense of completion. She felt that the moment was coming – in fact it was rushing towards her – to find a way to say goodbye to them. It was a kind of compulsion to think, for the moment, in an imminent way, and Marcia knew that when her thinking presented itself as ideas, and the ideas as words, the contraction of the fullness would make the world a toy. In reality everything was becoming tiny. The street itself showed her this: all the light of the street lamps did was reduce the night to a kind of protective bubble from which it was impossible to escape, as if from a dream. With a gesture very common in all those leaving an enclosed space, she raised her eyes to the sky (to see if it was raining). She seemed to see the stars; or saw them but absent-mindedly, without thinking, which when it comes to stars was the same as not seeing them at all. Not much time had passed, because the activity in the street had not changed since they had gone into the Pumper. Most of the youths were still standing on the opposite pavement; on this side there were small groups on the steps of the bank next to the Pumper, but mostly everything was in movement. The traffic was so dense it made your head spin. The punks' rapid steps, which for some unknown reason she fell in with, only added to this sensation. The crush of people separated and then brought them back together two or three times within a few metres. Mao took her by the arm impatiently, and pulled her towards the triangular recess of a perfume shop. Lenin followed them.

'Wanna fuck? Say you do.'

'Let go of me,' said Marcia, frowning. 'Start by taking your hands off me. The answer is no. It's still no: why would it change? I want to go home.'

And yet she had come to a halt. But when she saw Mao's determined gesture, one she thought was crazy – shaking her head without taking her eyes off Marcia's (normally when somebody shakes their head to say no, they take their eyes off the other person), she felt an urgent need to carry on walking. She could do this. Taking a few steps back towards the pavement, she paused to collect her thoughts. Alongside the desire to get away came a more powerful urge to talk, because she suddenly was able to, as if Mao's return to her main aim freed her from a spell.

'It was your fault we couldn't talk in there. We're in the same position as before, or worse. I wanted to know something, but I still don't have any idea about it. It may not be important to you, but what about me?'

'It's not important to you either.'

'You're so stubborn! And inconsiderate!'

'We did as you wanted, but in fact there was no need to talk.'

'In that case, there's nothing more to say. Bye.'

She set off without looking back at them.

'Love isn't something to be talked about,' said Mao.

'There are lots of things that can be talked about. It's all very complicated.' Marcia had no idea what she was saying.

'No, it's very simple. You have to decide on the spot.'

The other two had also started walking, very quickly as usual. The three of them were heading for the street corner. Mao seemed to be gathering strength for a decisive attack. Marcia decided she was no longer interested. She was fed up with the argument.

Far more than she admitted, Marcia was most sincerely disappointed that the conversation had got nowhere. Not so much because she had not learnt anything about the world of punks (as she had no idea what information there was, she couldn't know if they had told her a lot or a little), but because the punk world had not turned out to be a backwards world, the symmetrical, looking-glass image of the real one, with all its values reversed. That would have been the simplest answer, one that would have left her satisfied. Marcia was a bit ashamed to admit this, because it was so childish, but she didn't want to make things any more difficult for herself. It was a missed opportunity; with it everything else was lost, and so she considered the matter closed.

They had reached the street corner; Mao came to a halt. She peered along Calle Bonorino, which was in darkness, then turned to Marcia.

'Let's go along here a bit. There's something I want to tell you.'

'No. There's nothing more to say.'

'There's just one more thing, Marcia, but it's fundamental. Isn't it unfair to cut me off when I'm finally going to tell you the most important thing of all? Because now I do want to talk to you about love.'

In spite of everything she had decided a moment earlier, Marcia was curious. She knew she would hear nothing new, but still she felt intrigued. This was the magic spell the punks had cast on her: they made her believe the world could be renewed. The disappointment was secondary. Although she was the one who felt disappointed, Marcia was one of those people who had the habit of disregarding themselves and evaluating the situation without taking themselves into account. So she followed Mao, and Lenin followed her. They didn't walk far. There was a dark stretch twenty metres further on beyond the lit shop windows of Harding's. The three of them huddled against the wall. Mao launched straight in, her voice urgent. She had her eyes fixed on Marcia, who in the dim light felt freer to return her gaze with what was for her an unusual intensity.

'Marcia, I'm not going to tell you again that you're wrong, because you must know that by now. The big mistake is the world of explanations you live in. Love is a way out of that mistake. An escape from that mistake. Why do you reckon I can't love you? Do you have an inferiority complex, like all fatties? No. And if you think you do, you're wrong about that too. My love has transformed you. That world of yours is contained within the real world, Marcia.

I'm going to take the trouble to explain a few things to you, but don't forget I'm talking about the real world, not the one of explanations. What's preventing you from responding to me? Two things: the suddenness and the fact that I'm a girl. I've nothing to say about the suddenness; you believe in love at first sight just as I do, and so does the rest of the world. That's a necessity. We can't do without that. Now, as to me being a girl and not a boy, a woman and not a man . . . You're horrified at us being so brutal, but it hasn't occurred to you that in the end that's all there is. In those same explanations you're always looking for, when it comes down to it, when it's the very last explanation, what's left but a naked, horrible clarity? Even men are that brutal, even if they are professors of philosophy, because underneath everything else there's the length and breadth of their pricks. That and nothing more. That's the reality. Of course it may take them many years and many miles to realise that; they can exhaust every single word beforehand, but it's all the same, however long they take, whether it takes them a lifetime to get there, or if they flash their dick at you before you've even crossed the street. We women have the wonderful advantage of being able to choose the long or short route. We can turn the world into a stroke of lightning, the blink of an eye.

But since we don't have dicks, we waste our brutality in contemplation. And yet . . . *there is* suddenness. An instant when the whole world becomes real, when it undergoes the most radical change: the world becomes world. That's staring us in the face, Marcia. That's when all politeness, all conversation has to stop. It's happiness, and that's what I'm offering you. You'd be the most stupid cow of all time if you didn't see that. Just think, there's so little separating you from your destiny. You only have to say yes.'

Marcia had twice before noticed something strange she could not define. Now she knew what it was. She understood, or put into words, something she had been aware of for a while, perhaps from the start: that Mao was beautiful. It struck you immediately. She was surprised she had not told herself so before now. She was the most beautiful girl she had ever seen. And more than that. To have a pretty face and harmonious features or an exquisite range of expressions was not that unusual among girls of her age. But Mao was much, much more. She went beyond whatever thoughts could be formulated about beauty: she was like the sun, like light.

And this wasn't an effect. It wasn't the kind of beauty discovered over a short or long time, out of habit or love or both these things together; it wasn't beauty seen through the lens of subjectivity or time. It was objective. It was real beauty. Marcia was sure of this because beauty had never meant much to her; she didn't even notice it or take it into account. Among her schoolmates there were several who could boast that they were perfect beauties. Compared to Mao, they were like illusions confronted with the real.

OK, she told herself, so that was Mao's 'secret weapon', and everything could be explained from that starting point. But at the same time, that wasn't an explanation. Because how could beauty be a secret?

'And yet,' Mao was saying, 'love also allows for one detour, just one: action. Because love, which cannot be explained, does in fact have *proofs*. Of course, these are not exactly procrastination, because proofs are the only thing love has. And however slow and complicated they may be, they are also instantaneous. These proofs are as valuable as love, not because they are the same or equivalent, but because they open a perspective onto another aspect of life: action.'

Marcia had paid no more attention to this part of Mao's speech than to what had come before. Her own reflections were also coming to a close: her thoughts and Mao's were like two parallel series, and this lent them a certain harmony. After verifying, or discovering, Mao's beauty, and still affected by an amazement she could not name, Marcia turned to look at Lenin. What had just happened let her see something she had not seen before. In a way, she had not looked them in the face before.

Lenin was no beauty. Or perhaps she was. She had a long, horsey face, and all her features (eyes, nose, mouth) seemed out of proportion, and haphazard. But in her entirety, she could not be called ugly. She was different. So different she made one think of a kind of beauty that might be appreciated in another civilisation. She was the opposite of Mao. In an exotic, primitive or directly extra-terrestrial court, her face could have been considered a living jewel, the realisation of an ideal. Generations of incestuous monarchs would have been needed to produce her, and this would have led to dynastic struggles, intrigues, kidnappings, knights in strange armour, castles on the top of inaccessible hills . . . Lenin too had something for Marcia to discover, which became real at that moment: the novelesque. There was also a deep-seated similarity to Mao: they were like the two faces of the same thing. Beauty and silence exploded in the night. Unlike the other transformations she thought she had perceived, which were a turning of the page, this was the transformation of the world into world. It was the height of strangeness, and

Marcia did not think she could go any further. She was right about this, because there were no more transformations; or rather, the situation took on the aspect and rhythm of one great transformation that was simultaneously still and dizzying. Marcia congratulated herself for having given them another chance, and even felt a retrospective, hypothetical fear: if she had done as she intended and gone home a few minutes earlier, she would have missed this discovery, which seemed to her fundamental. How often, she thought, from not making one more tiny effort, people lost the opportunity for positive and enriching lessons.

Mao was looking expectantly at her. Marcia looked back at her and had to shut her eyes (inwardly): she was too beautiful. She was on the verge of asking her to please repeat the question, if there had been a question, but Mao wasn't expecting a reply. On the contrary, it was as if she herself gave it:

'You'll have to prove yourself,' she said.

Marcia had no idea what she was talking about, but nodded anyway. Then something extraordinary happened: Mao smiled. This was the first and only time she did so, and Marcia, who had absolutely no way of verifying that this was a smile, knew beyond the shadow of a doubt that Mao had smiled at her.

In fact this was one of the rarest phenomena in the universe, the 'serious smile', which men who are very lucky get to see once or twice in their lifetimes, and women practically never. It made her think, possibly by an association of names, of a photograph of Mao Tse-tung, one of those official photos in a blurred reproduction in a newspaper, where even with the best will in the world not even the keenest eye can decide whether there is or not the hint of a smile on the Chinese leader's face.

It was extremely fleeting, no more than an instant, and the punks were already off in search of their enigmatic 'proof'. Marcia gravitated to them naturally . . . the gravitational pull of mystery, still lost in the mist of her thoughts, none of which (neither the one about beauty, nor the one about the novelesque, nor about the smile) had assumed a definite shape. They crossed the street without bothering to look whether a car was coming or not; on the far corner the darkness was deeper because it was an abandoned arcade. After a moment's hesitation when Mao headed towards Rivadavia, she changed her mind and said something to Lenin.

'Let's go!' she ordered, and strode off in the opposite direction. Marcia had heard them mutter the word *Disco*, and from the way it was said had understood they were going to the supermarket of that name. And yes, passing the cinema and a small bakery, they went into an arcade at the end of which was the enormous Disco supermarket, all lit up in neon. She had an intuition of what they were planning. As far as proofs of love went it was a classic gesture (a classic even though nobody had done it for her before): to steal something from a supermarket and give it to her. The equivalent of what in olden days would have been the slaying of a dragon. Of course, she had no idea what it would prove, but she was ready to watch. Viewed from this century's enlightened present, anybody would say that dragons had never existed. But then again, for a medieval peasant, did supermarkets exist? In the same way, the proof that was still some distant possibility laid open the credit of existence. Would they ask her to wait outside? There were two massive glass walls separating the supermarket from the arcade. A lot of people were inside; all the tills were open, and there were long queues snaking between the displays and blocking everything. The main door was almost at the exit of the arcade on to Calle Camacuá. No, they weren't going to make her wait outside: without a word, Mao stepped aside so that Marcia could go in first. When she entered . . . Not exactly the moment she entered, but when she looked back and saw what

Lenin was doing when she came in . . . it was like the onset of a dream. And at the same time as if reality was starting.

From her bag, or possibly from among the metal objects hanging round her neck, Lenin had taken a heavy black iron padlock; she was closing the glass door, slipping the bolt and attaching the padlock. The click it made as it snapped shut made Marcia jump. It was as if the lock had literally shut on her heart. Or better still, as if her heart were the black iron padlock that was slightly rusty but still worked perfectly, too well in fact. Because the move had something irreversible about it (when a padlock closes it's as if it will never be able to be opened again, as if the key had somehow already been lost). Added to the surprise, this made it a dream come true . . .

She was not the only one to have seen this. A short, elderly woman with white hair and a red coat had just reached the door to go out, pushing a piled-high trolley.

'Get back,' Lenin told her, switch-blade open in her palm.

A boy in a Disco T-shirt who was helping load bags at the counter, had taken a few steps towards the intruder, but came to a halt when he saw the knife, his face almost comically reflecting his stupefaction. Lenin turned towards him, brandishing the blade:

'Stay still, you arsehole, or I'll kill you!' she shouted. And to the old woman, who was rooted to the spot: 'Get back to the till.'

She stamped her foot on the ground, then with a swift movement stabbed at a sachet of milk that was on top of the trolley. A jet of white spattered several other women approaching the exit right in the eyes.

Almost at once, Lenin moved beside Marcia towards the Fruit and Veg section, which gave on to the street. A man in a white apron came out from behind the electronic weighing machine, as if he had taken control of the situation and was determined to put a stop to it. Lenin wasted no time on him. She thrust the knife at him, and when the man raised his arms to snatch it from her or to hit her, she slashed his face at lightning speed. The blade slit his cheek down to the bone, from the gum behind his upper lip, from left cheek to right. His whole top lip was left dangling, with blood spurting up and down. He had begun to shout something, but never finished whatever it was. He raised both hands to his mouth.

All this had only taken a few seconds, scarcely long enough for anyone to realise what was happening. The women who were choosing fruit and vegetables in this section, from where the rest of the supermarket could not be seen, started to look over, to be alarmed, but Lenin was already trotting through them, knife dripping blood, towards the small counter at the back, where the girl receiving empty bottles stood rooted to the spot. Behind her was a small door which led to the delivery bay for trucks. Marcia, who had stayed near the front door, turned to get a better look at what Lenin was up to. She saw that she was heading for this other exit, to do the same as she had with the first one. This time it must be a metal shutter. She didn't doubt for a second that Lenin would lock it with another padlock . . . Marcia simply hoped she had the keys, because otherwise she had no idea how they would get out of there, and in this situation the need to get out was uppermost in her mind; she couldn't think of anything else. But somehow what would most characterise them, the inevitable, what was most like their way of burning bridges, was for there to be no keys, was that they were closing the padlocks forever.

At that moment, gunshots rang out over her head. Two, three or four of them: impossible to count. They were not all that loud, but the faces of those already alarmed snapped back. Incredibly, as yet, no one was shouting. To Marcia's left, against the walls giving on to the street and behind the electronic weighing machine, stood a ladder. All this area had a low ceiling. Up above hung a not very large goldfish bowl-cum-office, where obviously a guard was posted who could see every part of the supermarket. There was no closed-circuit TV or anything of the kind; the surveillance was on a primitive level, watchtower-style. Mao must have climbed the ladder while her friend was putting on the show with her knife, and by now must have overpowered the security guard. Overpowered or something worse: Marcia could have sworn he had not been the one to shoot.

In the deathly silence reigning in the Fruit and Veg section following the shots (all that could be heard through the loudspeakers was a jingle for instant mashed potato) the noise of the metal shutter to the adjacent delivery bay made a huge clang. It was such a conclusive sound that the padlock seemed unnecessary. To anyone else it would have seemed incredible that two young women could do things like shutting a metal shutter weighing tons, sidelining the dozen beefy truck drivers and porters who must have been in the delivery bay, or taking out one or two professional security guards and seizing their weapons . . . But to Marcia it did not seem unbelievable; on the contrary, she wouldn't have believed anything else.

The echo of the metal shutter slamming had scarcely faded away (really, these girls didn't allow anyone's attention to wander) when all gazes turned up to stare at the office suspended under the ceiling, where one of the glass panels had exploded. A hail of big and small shards of glass rained down on the aisle between Fruit and Veg and Soft Drinks. In the midst of them fell the projectile that had caused the damage, which was nothing other than a telephone, its cable torn out.

Meanwhile, panic had set in among customers and staff. This was only to be expected, because time does not pass in vain. Some had started shouting; others had seriously begun to contemplate the thought of getting out. Quite a few were heading for the exit, and those already there were rattling the door vigorously but to no avail. There was nothing they could do: to get out they would have to smash the glass. That would not have been too difficult, or even complicated (especially considering this could have avoided what seemed like an imminent bloodbath), and yet it's incredible the superstitious respect a large pane of glass can arouse. And a few seconds later, when common sense prevailed, it would be too late.

Marcia, whom no one had noticed, huddled with the others by the door. From there she had a view of the whole supermarket. She had no idea if it was luck or careful calculation that had helped the punks during the first phase of the operation. The entrance door, the steps up to the office, the way to the store-room, were all concealed behind the big Fruit and Veg display, which separated the narrow strip next to the street from the rest of the space. From there, the first visible sign that something was going on was the smashing of the glass in the hanging office. The supermarket floor was quite big, some forty metres long by thirty wide. Those at the far end might have thought it was an accident. Some might not even have heard or seen it. The loudspeakers were still pouring out adverts for oil and crackers. Soon, very soon, any room for doubt would disappear.

That was when Mao appeared in the hole created by the broken glass, revolver in one hand and micro-phone in the other. She looked calm, self-assured, an imposing figure, in no hurry. Above all, in no hurry, because she wasn't wasting a single moment. Things were happening in a packed continuum which they had perfect control of. It was as if there were two distinct times operating simultaneously: the one the two punks were in, doing one thing after another without any pause or waiting, and the other of the spectator-victims, where everything was pauses and waiting. The recording that had been coming over the loudspeakers had stopped, replaced by the sound of Mao breathing as she prepared to speak. This in itself caused widespread terror. Efficiency often has that effect. It must have been quite simple to cut the transmission of a recorded tape and replace it with a directly amplified voice: no more than pushing a button. But knowing how to do something easy is not easy. The entire clientele of the supermarket joining forces could have been pushing buttons for a whole week without succeeding. And they knew this, which made them feel they were at the mercy of an efficiency that asserted itself so effortlessly.

'Listen carefully, all of you,' said Mao over all the loudspeakers in the store. She spoke slowly, carefully controlling the echoes. She had adopted a neutral tone, as though giving information, but it was pure hysteria. So great and pure that the growing hysteria among the customers of both sexes seemed like nothing more than an everyday attack of nerves. It led them to understand that it was not enough for their nervousness or fears to pile up and grow in order to become hysteria. This was something different. It was something that by defini- tion did not grow, a paroxysm reached outside life, in madness or fiction. As silence fell, the beeps from the last tills that had continued to work died away.

'This supermarket has been taken over by the Love Commando. If you collaborate, there will not be many injured or dead. There will be some, because Love is demanding. The number depends on you. We will take all the money in the tills, and then leave. Within a quarter of an hour, the survivors will be at home watching TV. That's all. Remember that everything that happens here, will be a proof of *love*.'

How literary she was! This was followed by one of those moments of hesitation that take place at the expense of the real in reality. A man in one of the queues guffawed. Immediately there was the sound of a gunshot, but instead of producing a hole in the forehead of the man who had laughed, the bullet hit the leg of a small woman who was two behind him in the queue. The leg began to spout blood, and the woman fainted melodramatically. A huge commotion and shouting. Mao waved the recently fired revolver and raised the microphone to her lips again. White and shaken, the man stopped laughing. The shot had been intended for him. It was as if he was dead, because in the fiction related to his earlier incredulity the bullet-hole really was in his forehead.

'Everybody back,' said Mao. 'Move away from the tills; you cashiers as well. Stand between the shelves. I'm going to get down now. I'm not going to give you any more warnings.' She tossed the revolver over her shoulder, using her free hand to feel for the things she was carrying round her neck. She picked out one, which looked like a small black metal pineapple, the size of a hen's egg. She said: 'This is a nerve gas grenade. If I let it off, you'll all be paralysed and brain-dead for the rest of your lives.'

There was a mass retreat. The people on the far side of the tills rushed through them. The cashiers abandoned their posts; supervisors, assistants, everyone piled up, trying to hide behind the shelves. Those who found the woman who had fainted was in their way trampled over her and the spreading pool of blood around her body. There must have been about four hundred people of all ages and social groups as well as quite a few children, some of them babies in pushchairs. They pushed and shoved in their haste to get away, but what Mao said next stopped them in their tracks.

'Look over there,' she said, pointing to her left. Lenin had appeared on top of the dairy counter, holding a bunch of petrol cans in her hand. 'Anyone trying to get out round the back of the displays will be burnt alive.'

The whole end wall of the store was covered with low meat freezers, a counter for cheeses and cold meats, and finally, separated by a narrow aisle, the milk and dairy fridge that Lenin was standing on. But beyond them was an empty area, in which employees of both sexes were stood in white aprons, staring in astonishment at the back of the arsonist, who wasn't paying them the slightest attention. Why didn't they go for her? Most of them had not learned of Lenin's locking the delivery bay, and might have thought it was still open, with people inside who could come to their aid. And so two men, one of them smaller, the other huge and with a big belly, rushed instinctively to grapple with Lenin, hoping to open a breach and head for the street exit. The fat guy, who must have thought he was a human locomotive, managed to climb up through the yogurts and reach out to the sentinel, who did not move. In the blink of an eye he was doused in petrol, and a well-aimed kick sent him sprawling on his back. He had barely touched the ground when he burst into flames. Had she thrown a match at him? Nobody really saw. By now he was a flaming torch. His plastic overall caught fire spectacularly, and his cries echoed all round the supermarket. He was hit on the head by another petrol can, and since this exploded on the spot, turning his brain into a fireball, he suddenly stopped screaming. Only slightly singed, his colleague did his best to hide among the others. Of all the shouts going up, it was curious that the most intelligible were those of the women who for their children's sake begged for the threat of gas not to be carried out. Some things strike a chord in the imagination.

While this was going on, all the lights had gone off, and the red numbers on the tills, and the sound system. From her perch, Mao had cut off the electricity. In the sudden darkness (their eyes would take a few seconds to adjust and take advantage of the light from the arcade and street) the effect of the burning man and the vast pool of flaming fuel was dazzling.

But the two attackers did not seem to have to wait to get used to the darkness. They had done so earlier, and now they only had to act. Like a bat or nocturnal monkey, Mao dropped down from the office to the first of the tills. She began to leap from one to the next until she reached the furthest one. Curious onlookers had started to gather in the shopping arcade on the other side of the windows. They peered in without understanding what was going on.

Beyond the displays and the customers, the tearful, baying crowd (after all, they had been told to follow orders, but not to be quiet), Lenin was moving in the opposite direction to her friend, along the tops of the freezers, treading on meat and chickens. If this movement were not simply carried out to create an impression of symmetry, it could have no other motive than to dissuade and threaten. Everything seemed aimed at that: there was a threat, but not a simple, straightforward and comprehensible one, rather one confused with the realities it referred to, which in this way no longer functioned as a language but merged in a blurred, illegible whole. And yet a language did exist, because in the bilateral symmetry of their manoeuvres Mao represented the ultimate intention: to steal the money from the tills, whereas Lenin was the threat that existed above and beyond their crimes, since she prevented any escape in the other direction. And she obviously did have something in mind, because she leant over and gathered together the trolleys close to the freezers and launched them towards the back of the store, towards the milk products and the wine shelves.

When she reached the last till, Mao began to empty it systematically. She did so without taking her feet from the conveyor belt, simply bending down from the waist. She pressed the button that released the cash drawer, tore out the tray containing different compartments for change, scooped up the large-denomination banknotes underneath, and stuffed them into a plastic bag dangling from her wrist. This operation took her no more than a second or two; then she jumped across to the next till.

She was leaping from the second to the third till
(and the spectators were only just beginning to realise
what was going on) when an explosion rocked the
supermarket, the arcade it was part of, the surrounding block, and doubtless the entire neighbourhood. By
some miracle, the panes of glass at the front were not
blown out, but something even better occurred: they
were shattered but stayed in place, turning opaque as
though covered in vapour, so thwarting the curiosity
of the onlookers outside – most of whom had run off
anyway when they heard the noise, fearing the whole
arcade might fall in. The hostages' terror reached new
heights. The explosion had come from the delivery
bay behind Lenin. It must have been caused by a fuel
tank. The sudden holes in the wall let in light and
the dreadful crackle of the fire. Almost immediately
there were another two explosions, perhaps from the
lorries' petrol tanks. Although less deafening than the
first, they were accompanied by the screech of bits of
metal tearing apart. The lights had gone out in the
arcade as well, so that now the scene was lit only by
the dancing, flickering flames. Mao had not paused,
and by now had emptied another two tills. If it crossed
anybody's mind to take advantage of the darkness
to grab her, they must have thought twice about it,
because the entire wall between the store and the

warehouse area now silently collapsed. Since everything was in flames on the far side, the whole scene was bathed in an intense glow. One person did not consider this properly, and threw herself at the thief. She was a girl in a cashier's pink uniform; a robust, stocky and obviously determined young woman. The sight of the fire had spurred her on, or had led her to forget the precautions of only a few seconds before. Maybe she thought her example would lead to a general revolt. But that didn't happen. She ran straight for Mao, who was leaning over a till. She charged like a rhinoceros, as if this were a natural instinct in her, almost as though she made a habit of it, as if in the past this manoeuvre had always brought good results. Mao's reaction was instantaneous and very precise: she swayed backwards, a bottle of wine in one hand, and brought it down in a wide arc at the very instant the chubby cashier reached her. It smashed on her forehead, and the crack of the poor girl's skull resounded round the store. It was a brutal death, but somehow in keeping with her bull-like charge. No one else tried to copy her. Despite this, Mao stopped what she was doing for a moment and surveyed the motionless crowd in among the shelves. The light from the fire shone directly on her. She was so beautiful it sent shivers down the spine.

'Don't interrupt me again!' was all she said.

She let another second go by, like a schoolteacher might do after reprimanding some unruly pupils, to see if there were any objection. The four hundred desperate hostages had none whatsoever. Without opening their mouths, they all seemed to be shouting: 'We don't want to die!'

But one shrill voice was raised among the mass of shadows where madness might well be brewing.

Although shrill, it was a man's voice. With a very strong Colombian accent. From the first few syllables, many of those present realised what was going on. The neighbourhood is itself an education. Two blocks from *Disco*, on the corner of Camacuá and Bonifacio, there was a Faculty of Theology that offered scholarships to students from all over Latin America. They stayed in apartments on the campus and shopped in the area. They were a kind of learned evangelist, with a touch of hippie. In a neighbourhood like Flores, foreigners are always suspected of being indiscreet. It was almost inevitable that this Colombian should intervene.

'You don't scare me, Satan!' he began. And that was practically it.

Lenin had interrupted her manoeuvres by the space between the displays where the voice was coming from. From the opposite direction to Mao, she was silhouetted against the flames, which were very close to her. In her hand a transparent petrol can shone like a gem. There were at least fifty people between her and the protestor, but that did not seem to deter her.

'Shut up, you idiot!' shouted one man. Shouts backing him up came from all around, demonstrating an unsuspected hatred of religion.

'The devil . . . ' shrieked the Colombian.

'What devil, for fuck's sake!'

'Shut up, why don't you?'

'Kill him, kill him!' a woman shouted. 'For our children's sake! Kill him before there's another tragedy!'

And another woman, more philosophical:

'This is no time for sermons!'

In reality, the Colombian had not even begun any religious argument, but the others had sensed it coming anyway. In a neighbourhood like Flores, everything is known. And what isn't known is intuited. The first man who had shouted him down started punching him. There was a tremendous uproar, because the student, who ought to have been feeble, a member of a decadent race, defended himself. But none of this was visible in the darkness. Besides, there were outbreaks of hysteria elsewhere in the crowd. A controlled, cautious hysteria, because no one wanted to overstep the boundaries the attackers had set.

Even so, it did not look as if those boundaries would be respected for more than a few seconds. The fire was really terrifying, and gave the impression it would soon spread to the store itself. Besides, if one wall had collapsed, the roof might come down as well. Mao had begun her looting of the tills again, but seemed to be doing so more slowly now, half-expecting an attack, almost wanting to teach them another lesson.

The reasonable thing would have been for her to finish taking the money, and then for the attackers to flee. Nobody was going to stop them. But their initial warning echoed in the collective consciousness: if they were doing all this for love, something was missing, some fresh horror. Love always could always do more.

In response to this plea, Lenin took a horrendous initiative. The tumult caused by the Colombian was still going on when the deafening sound of a trolley was heard, launched like a missile from one end to the other of the back aisle. Those close to it could see the trolley was filled to the brim with bottles of champagne, and topped off with half a dozen jerry-cans of petrol and an areola of blue flames. It sped straight down the aisle without touching anything, and crashed into one end of the soft drinks display. The blast was unparalleled; the shock wave a dense mass of splinters of green glass and flaming alcohol. The impact also set off the rapid explosion of a thousand soft drinks bottles. A lot of people had sought refuge in among these shelves, and so the accident caused even greater chaos. It was as if the screams were reaching the highest heavens. Mao's movement between the tills had become supernaturally slow.

The confusion was so great it would be a shame not to take advantage of it, thought one woman who found herself in a convenient spot. She must have thought: what are we waiting for? If this is a nightmare, let's behave the way we do in dreams. Mao had advanced across six or seven tills already. She was a long way from the first ones, and that must have settled it as far as this impatient woman was concerned. She sprinted as fast as she could from the displays to the gap between the first and second till. She raced through and in the blink of an eye was up against the window giving on to the arcade. If she had put her shoulder to it, she would have got out: it was only by some miracle or other that the completely shattered glass had stayed in place, and it would not have resisted a determined shove. But the woman, either stunned or crazy, wanted to take the logic of dreams that had got her this far to its inevitable conclusion: kneeling down in front of the plate-glass window, she began cutting it with the diamond in her ring. The circle she started to trace was far too small for her body, but that was the least of her problems. In two bounds, Mao had come up behind her, and nobody saw exactly what she did among the madly dancing shadows. It barely lasted an instant. In the first half of this short lapse of time, the woman managed to scream loudly; in the second, supreme half she fell quiet, and with good reason. When her attacker straightened up, like a modern Salomé dressed in black, she was holding the woman's head in her hands. The spectacle had attracted everyone's attention. The hubbub intensified, and what emerged out of it, more than the cries of 'Murderer!' 'Animal!' and so on, were the 'Don't look!' that everybody was urging everyone else to do. This was the second half of what was dreamt: the fear of dreaming, or of remembering, which is the same thing. But Mao had leapt up onto the till closest to her, and threw the head like a bowling ball at the shouting crowd.

As the severed head traced an arc through the air in which all the brutal light and darkness of the fire was vividly etched, a second trolley behind the backs of the spectators was despatched in the opposite direction to the first. A fresh blast set off a third fire against the back wall of the store, where the thoughtful shelves of wine were kept. It became impossible to breathe, as the fire's intense heat was filled with acrid smells. Everything edible or drinkable in the supermarket was added to the concoction. The household cleaning department adjacent to the soft drinks area had also caught fire. The containers of solvents, waxes, polishes and ammonia went up with a choking stench. The trapped crowds tried to get away, trampling on each other, showing no solidarity, each one desperate to save themself. Whole displays began to give way on top of people. And the woman's head was still in mid-air, not because it had come to a standstill in a miraculous postmortem levitation, but because only a very short space of time had elapsed.

In the darkness of the flames, in the crystal of smoke and blood, the scene was multiplied in a thousand images, and each of these thousand in a thousand more . . . realms of weightless, rootless gold. It was as if at last there was a kind of understanding of what was going on. There is an old proverb which says: If God does not exist, everything is permitted. But the fact is that everything is never permitted, because there are laws of verisimilitude that survive the Creator. Even so, the second part of the proverb can function, that is, become reality, hypothetically at least, giving rise to a second proverb on the same lines as the original: If everything is permitted . . . This new proverb does not have a second part. Indeed, if everything is permitted . . . then what? This question was projected onto the thousand confused contours of the panic in the supermarket, and found some sort of reply. If everything is permitted . . . everything is transformed. It is true that transformation is also a question; on this occasion however, it became a momentary, shifting affirmation; it did not matter that it was still an interrogative, it was also an answer. The incident had illuminated, even if in the shadows, the amazing potential for transformation latent in all things. A woman, for example, a local housewife who had gone to buy food for supper, was melting on the spot in full view of her neighbours, who paid no attention to her. The fire had caught the viscose of her padded coat, and she had turned into a monster, but a dancing monster, lending her a voluptuousness she had never possessed when she was alive. Her limbs were elongated – one hand at the end of a three-metre long arm was crawling across the floor, a leg twisted and twisted endlessly on itself like a cobra . . . And she was singing, without opening her mouth, in a voice that would have left Maria Callas sounding flatulent and fuzzy, while at the same time the song was enriched by inhuman laughter, panting and prancing . . . she became animal, but all animals at once, an animal spectacle, with the bars of her cage sticking out like spines from every fold of her body, an animal jungle weighed down with orchids. A torrential rainbow spread over her: red, blue, snow white, green, dark gloomy green . . . She became vegetable, a stone, a stone colliding, the sea, an octopus automaton . . . she murmured, acted (Rebecca, an unforgettable woman), declaiming her lines while also a mime artist, a planet, a crackling sweet wrapper, an active and passive expression in Japanese . . . and at the same time she was no more than a gaze, a tiny insistence. Because the same thing could happen to anyone, and in fact did so; she was only one instance among hundreds, a picture at an exhibition.

Mao was still busy and either because she had been so diligent or because the time had arrived, she was coming to the end of the tills. The bag she was holding in her left hand was stuffed with money. How much time had elapsed? Five minutes in total since they had burst into the supermarket? And so much had happened! They were all waiting for the police or the firemen, but knew this was merely an atavistic habit, because there was nothing to wait for. What they felt was the opposite of someone coming to help: the general atmosphere was a centrifugal force, the Big Bang, the birth of the universe. It was as if everything known were dispersing at the speed of light, to create in the far distance, in the blackness of the universe, new civilisations based on other premises.

It was a beginning, but also the end. Because Mao, her job done, leapt down from the first till, and Lenin joined her. Together, the two of them threw themselves at the corner of the window giving onto the street with the untouchable force of love. The glass shattered and they vanished cleanly through the hole . . . two boundless dark shapes swallowed up by the immensity of the world outside . . . and at the very moment they disappeared, a third shadow joined them . . . Three stars whirling in the vast rotation of the night . . . the Three Marias that all the children of the southern hemisphere peer up at, spellbound, uncomprehending . . . and were lost on the streets of Flores.

27th May 1989

Dear readers,

As well as relying on bookshop sales, And Other Stories relies on subscriptions from people like you to tell these other stories – stories that other publishers often consider too risky to take on.

All of our subscribers:

- receive a first-edition copy of each of the books they subscribe to
- are thanked by name at the end of our subscriber-supported books
- receive little extras from us by way of thank you, for example: postcards created by our authors

BECOME A SUBSCRIBER, OR GIVE A SUBSCRIPTION TO A FRIEND

Visit andotherstories.org/subscribe to help make our books happen. You can subscribe to books we're in the process of making. To purchase books we have already published, we urge you to support your local or favourite bookshop and order directly from them – the often unsung heroes of publishing.

OTHER WAYS TO GET INVOLVED

If you'd like to know about upcoming events and reading groups (our foreign language reading groups help us choose books to publish, for example) you can:

- join the mailing list at: andotherstories.org/join-us
- follow us on Twitter: @andothertweets
- join us on Facebook: facebook.com/AndOtherStoriesBooks
- follow our blog: andotherstoriespublishing.tumblr.com

This book was made possible thanks to the support of:

Aaron McEnery · Aaron Schneider · Ada Gokay · Adam Bowman · Adam Lenson · Aileen-Elizabeth Taylor · Ailsa Peate · Ajay Sharma · Alan McMonagle · Alan Ramsey · Alasdair Hutchison · Alasdair Thomson · Alastair Gillespie · Alastair Laing · Alex Collinson · Alex Fleming · Alex Ramsey · Alexandra Citron · Alexandra de Verseg-Roesch · Ali Conway · Ali Smith · Alice Brett · Alice Firebrace · Alice Nightingale · Alison Hughes · Alison Layland · Alison Lock · Alison MacConnell · Alison Winston · Allison Graham · Alyse Ceirante · Amanda · Amanda Dalton · Amber Da · Amelia Ashton · Amelia Dowe · Ami Zarchi · Amine Hamadache · Amitav Hajra · Amy McDonnell · Andrew Gummerson · Andrew Kerr-Jarrett · Andrew Marston · Andrew Rego · Andrew Wilkinson · Angela Brant · Angela Creed ·

Angela Everitt · Anna Ball · Anna Corrigan · Anna Glendenning · Anna Milsom · Anna-Maria Aurich · Anne Carus · Anne Frost · Anne Ryden · Anne Stokes · Annie McDermott · Anonymous · Anonymous · Anonymous · Anthony Carrick · Anthony Quinn · Antonia Lloyd-Jones · Antonio de Swift · Antonio Garcia · Antony Pearce · Aoife Boyd · Archie Davies · Asako Serizawa · Asher Norris · Ashley Hamilton · Audrey Mash · Avril Joy · Avril Marren · Barbara Adair · Barbara Mellor · Barbara Robinson · Barry John Fletcher · Beatriz St. John · Becky Woolley · Ben Schofield · Ben Thornton · Benjamin Judge · Bernard Devaney · Beth Hore · Bianca Jackson · Bianca Winter · Bill Fletcher · Bill Myers · Bosun Smee · Brandon Knibbs · Branka Maricic · Brenda Sully · Brendan McIntyre · Briallen Hopper · Brigid

Maher · Brigita Ptackova · Caitlyn Chappell · Callie Steven · Candida Lacey · Caren Harple · Carl Emery · Carla Carpenter · Carla Shedivy · Carol McKay · Carolina Pineiro · Caroline Maldonado · Caroline Paul · Caroline Picard · Caroline Smith · Caroline West · Cassidy Hughes · Catherine Edwards · Catherine Taylor · Catriona Gibbs · Cecilia Uribe · Cecily Maude · Charles Raby · Charlie Laing · Charlotte Holtam · Charlotte Ryland · Charlotte Whittle · Charlotte Murrie & Stephen Charles · Chia Foon Yeow · China Miéville · Chris Ball · Chris Gribble · Chris Lintott · Chris McCann · Chris Nielsen · Chris & Kathleen Repper-Day · Chris Stevenson · Christine Brantingham · Christine Luker · Christopher Allen · Christopher Terry · Ciara Ní Riain · Claire Riley · Claire Trevien · Claire Tristram · Claire

Williams · Clarissa Botsford · Claudia Hoare · Claudia Nannini · Clifford Posner · Clive Bellingham · Colin Burrow · Colin Matthews · Colin Tucker · Courtney Lilly · Craig Aitchison · Dan Walpole · Daniel Arnold · Daniel Gallimore · Daniel Gillespie · Daniel Hahn · Daniel Rice · Daniel Stewart · Daniel Venn · Daniela Steierberg · Darcy Hurford · Dave Lander · Dave Young · Davi Rocha · David Finlay · David Hebblethwaite · David Higgins · David Johnson-Davies · David Miller · David Shriver · David Smith · David Travis · Debbie Pinfold · Declan O'Driscoll · Denis Stillewagt and Anca Fronescu · Derek Smith · Dominick Santa Cattarina · Dominique Brocard · E Rodgers · Ed Owles · Ed Tallent · Edward Haxton · Elaine Rassaby · Eleanor Dawson · Eleanor Maier · Elie Howe · Elise Gilbert · Eliza O'Toole · Elizabeth Cochrane ·

Elizabeth Heighway · Ellen Coopersmith · Ellen Kennedy · Ellie Goddard · Elsbeth Julie Watering · Emile Bojesen · Emily Diamand · Emily McLean-Inglis · Emily Taylor · Emily Williams · Emily Yaewon Lee & Gregory Limpens · Emma Bielecki · Emma Louise Grove · Emma Perry · Emma Teale · Emma Timpany · Emma Turesson · Erin Louttit · Eva Kostyu · Ewan Tant · Fawzia Kane · Felicity Box · Finbarr Farragher · Fiona Graham · Fiona Malby · Fiona Quinn · Fran Sanderson · Frances Hazelton · Francis Taylor · Francisco Vilhena · Frank van Orsouw · Freya Warren · Friederike Knabe · Gabriela Lucia Garza de Linde · Gabrielle Crockatt · Gale Pryor · Gary Dickson · Gary Gorton · Gavin Collins · Gawain Espley · Geoff Thrower · Geoffrey Cohen · Geoffrey Fisher · Geoffrey Fletcher · Geoffrey Urland · George McCaig · George Sandison &

Daniela Laterza · George Wilkinson · Georgia Panteli · Gerard Mehigan · Gerry Craddock · Gill Boag-Munroe · Gillian Grant · Gillian Spencer · Gina Dark · Glen Bornais · Gordon Cameron · Graham Mash · Graham R Foster · Grant Hartwell · Grant Rintoul · Guy Haslam · Hadil Balzan · Hank Pryor · Hannah Jones · Hans Lazda · Harriet Mossop · Heather Tipon · Helen Asquith · Helen Barker · Helen Brady · Helen Collins · Helen Weir · Helen Wormald · Helene Walters-Steinberg · Henriette Heise · Henrike Laehnemann · Henry Asson · Henry Hitchings · HL Turner-Heffer · Howard Robinson · Hugh Gilmore · Ian Barnett · Ian McMillan · Ian Randall · Ian Stephen · Ingrid Olsen · Irene Mansfield · Isabella Livorni · Isabella Weibrecht · Isobel Dixon · J Collins · Jack Brown · Jacqueline Haskell · Jacqueline Lademann · Jacqueline Ting Lin · Jacqueline

Vint · Jakob Hammarskjöld · James Attlee · James Butcher · James Clark · James Cubbon · James Lesniak · James Portlock · James Scudamore · James Tierney · James Ward · Jamie Mollart · Jamie Walsh · Jane Woollard · Janette Ryan · Jasmin Kate Kirkbride · Jasmine Gideon · Jean-Jacques Regouffre · Jeff Collins · Jeffrey Davies · Jen Campbell · Jennifer Bernstein · Jennifer Higgins · Jennifer Humbert · Jennifer Hurstfield · Jennifer O'Brien · Jenny Huth · Jenny Newton · Jenny Nicholls · Jeremy Faulk · Jeremy Weinstock · Jess Howard-Armitage · Jessie Eames · Jethro Soutar · JG Williams · Jim Boucherat · Jim McAuliffe · Jo Bellamy · Jo Harding · Jo Lateu · Joan Cornish · Joanna Flower · Joanna Luloff · Joao Pedro Bragatti Winckler · Jodie Adams · Jodie Hare · Jodie Lewis · Joel Love · Joelle Delbourgo · Johan Forsell · Johanna Eliasson · Johannes Menzel · Johannes

Georg Zipp · John Conway · John Gent · John Hodgson · John Kelly · John McKee · John Royley · John Shaw · John Steigerwald · John Winkelman · Jon Riches · Jon Talbot · Jonathan Blaney · Jonathan Jackson · Jonathan Ruppin · Jonathan Watkiss · Joseph Cooney · Joseph Schreiber · Joseph Zanella · Joshua Davis · Joshua McNamara · Julia Hays · Julia Hobsbawm · Julia Rochester · Julian Duplain · Julian Lomas · Julie Arscott · Julie Gibson · Julie Gibson · Juliet Swann · Kaarina Hollo · Kapka Kassabova · Karen Faarbaek de Andrade Lima · Karin Sehmer · Katarina Trodden · Kate Attwooll · Kate Gardner · Kate Griffin · Kate Pullinger · Katharina Liehr · Katharine Freeman · Katharine Robbins · Katherine El-Salahi · Katherine Green · Katherine Mackinnon · Katherine Parish · Katherine Skala · Katherine Sotejeff-Wilson · Kathleen Magone · Kathleen

Sargeant · Kathryn Edwards · Kathryn Lewis · Katie Brown · Katja Bell · Katrina Thomas · Katy Bircher · Kay Pluke · Keith Walker · Kent McKernan · Khairunnisa Ibrahim · Kirsten Major · KL Ee · Klara Rešetič · Kristin Djuve · Krystine Phelps · Lana Selby · Lance Anderson · Lander Hawes · Laura Batatota · Laura Brown · Laura Lea · Laura Renton · Laura Willett · Lauren Ellemore · Laurence Laluyaux · Leanne Bass · Leeanne O'Neill · Leigh Vorhies · Leonie Schwab · Leonie Smith · Lesley Lawn · Lesley Watters · Liliana Lobato · Lindsay Brammer · Lindsey Ford · Lindsey Stuart · Lindy van Rooyen · Linnea Frank · Liz Clifford · Liz Ketch · Liz Wilding · Lizzi Thomson · Lizzie Broadbent · Lochlan Bloom · Loretta Platts · Lorna Bleach · Lottie Smith · Louise Musson · Luc Verstraete · Lucia Rotheray · Lucy Caldwell · Lucy Hariades · Lucy Moffatt · Luke Healey · Lydia

Bruton-Jones · Lynn Martin · M Manfre · Madalena Alfaia · Maeve Lambe · Magdalena Choluj · Maggie Humm · Maggie Livesey · Maggie Redway · Mahan L Ellison & K Ashley Dickson · Maisie Gibson · Malcolm Ramsay · Margaret Briggs · Margaret Jull Costa · Marie Bagley · Marie Donnelly · Marina Castledine · Marina Jones · Mark Dawson · Mark Lumley · Mark Sargent · Mark Waters · Marlene Adkins · Martha Gifford · Martha Nicholson · Martha Stevns · Martin Brampton · Martin Price · Martin Vosyka · Martin Whelton · Mary Carozza · Mary Cox · Mary Wang · Matt & Owen Davies · Matthew Armstrong · Matthew Black · Matthew Francis · Matthew Smith · Matthew Thomas · Matty Ross · Maureen Pritchard · Maurice Maguire · Max Longman · Meaghan Delahunt · Megan Wittling · Melissa Beck · Melissa Quignon-Finch · Merima Jahic ·

Meryl Wingfield · Michael Aguilar · Michael Andal · Michael Holtmann · Michael Johnston · Michael Moran · Michael Ward · Michael John Garcés · Michelle Roberts · Midge Gillies · Milo Waterfield · Mitchell Albert · Monika Olsen · Morgan Lyons · MP Boardman · Namita Chakrabarty · Nancy Foley · Nancy Oakes · Naomi Kruger · Natalie Smith · Natalie Steer · Nathalie Atkinson · Nathan Loceff · Neil Pretty · Nia Emlyn-Jones · Nicholas Brown · Nick Chapman · Nick Flegel · Nick James · Nick Nelson & Rachel Eley · Nick Rombes · Nick Sidwell · Nicola Hart · Nicola Sandiford · Nicole Matteini · Nikolaj Ramsdal Nielsen · Nina Alexandersen · Nina de la Mer · Nina Power · Noelle Harrison · Nuala Watt · Octavia Kingsley · Olga Zilberbourg · Olivia Payne · Olivier Pynn · Pamela Ritchie · Pashmina Murthy · Pat Crowe · Patricia Appleyard · Patricia Hughes · Patrick

McGuinness · Patrick Owen · Paul Bailey · Paul Cray · Paul Daw · Paul Fulcher · Paul Griffiths · Paul Jones · Paul Munday · Paul Myatt · Paul Segal · Paula Edwards · Paula Ely · Penelope Hewett Brown · Peter McCambridge · Peter Rowland · Peter Vilbig · Peter Vos · Philip Carter · Philip Nulty · Philip Warren · Philippa Wentzel · Phyllis Reeve · Piet Van Bockstal · PM Goodman · Portia Msimang · PRAH Foundation · Rachael Savill · Rachael Williams · Rachel Beddow · Rachel Carter · Rachel Hinkel · Rachel Lasserson · Rachel Parkin · Rachel Van Riel · Rachel Wadham · Rachel Watkins · Rea Cris · Read MAW Books · Rebecca Braun · Rebecca Carter · Rebecca Moss · Rebecca Rosenthal · Réjane Collard-Walker · Rhiannon Armstrong · Richard Ashcroft · Richard Dew · Richard Ellis · Richard Gwyn · Richard Priest · Richard Ross · Richard Shea · Rishi Dastidar · Robert

Gillett · Robert
Hugh-Jones · Robert
Norman · Robin Cooley
· Robin Patterson ·
Robin Taylor · Ros
Schwartz · Rose Arnold
· Rosie Pinhorn · Roz
Simpson · Rufus
Johnstone · Rune
Salvesen · Ruth Parkin ·
Sabine Griffiths · Sally
Baker · Sally Foreman ·
Sam Gordon · Sam
Norman · Sam Ruddock
· Sam Stern · Samantha
Sabbarton-Wright ·
Samantha Sawers ·
Samantha Smith ·
Sandra Neilson · Sarah
Benson · Sarah
Blakeman · Sarah
Butler · Sarah Jacobs ·
Sarah Lippek · Sarah
Lucas · Sarah Pybus ·
Sarah Salmon · Scott
Thorough · Sean Kelly ·
Sean Malone · Sean
McGivern · Seini
O'Connor · Sergio
Gutierrez Negron · Sez
Kiss · Shannon Knapp ·
Shaun Whiteside ·
Shawn Moedl ·
Sheridan Marshall ·
Shirley Harwood · Sian
O'Neill · Simon
Armstrong · Simon
Clark · Simone
O'Donovan · Sioned
Puw Rowlands · Siriol
Hugh-Jones · SJ Bradley

· Sonia McLintock ·
Sophia Wickham ·
Soren Murhart ·
Srikanth Reddy · ST
Dabbagh · Stacy
Rodgers · Stefanie
Barschdorf · Stefanie
May IV · Steph Morris ·
Stephanie Lacava ·
Stephen Pearsall ·
Steven & Gitte Evans ·
Stu Sherman · Stuart
Wilkinson · Sue Little ·
Susan Higson · Susan
Irvine · Susie Roberson
· Suzanne Lee ·
Swannee Welsh · Sylvie
Zannier-Betts · Tamara
Larsen · Tammi Owens
· Tammy Harman ·
Tammy Watchorn ·
Tania Hershman ·
Tehmina Khan · Teresa
Griffiths · Terry Kurgan
· The Mighty Douche
Softball Team · The
Rookery In the Bookery
· Thomas Bell · Thomas
Fritz · Thomas
O'Rourke · Thomas van
den Bout · Tim Jackson
· Tim Theroux ·
Timothy Harris · Tina
Andrews · Tina
Rotherham-Winqvist ·
TJ Clark · Toby Ryan ·
Tom Darby · Tom
Franklin · Tom Gray ·
Tom Johnson · Tom
Ketteley · Tom Mandall
· Tom Wilbey · Tony

Bastow · Torna
Russell-Hills · Tracy
Heuring · Tracy
Northup · Trevor Lewis
· Trevor Wald · Val
Challen · Vanessa
Nolan · Veronica
Cockburn · Vicky Grut ·
Victoria Adams ·
Victoria Walker · Vilis
Kasims · Virginia Weir ·
Visaly Muthusamy ·
Wendy Langridge ·
Wendy Olson · Wenna
Price · Will Huxter ·
Will Nash & Claire
Meiklejohn · William
Dennehy · William
Mackenzie · Zoë Brasier

'Reading him is dizzying.'
The Guardian
THE LITTLE BUDDHIST MONK
César Aira

'Hail César!' Patti Smith

THE SEAMSTRESS AND THE WIND

César Aira